Brutal

A Revenge Marriage Troubles Dark Mafia Romance

Struck In Love
Book 4

Chiquita Dennie

304 Publishing Company

Disclaimer

This is a fast paced novella, introduces new characters.This work of fiction contains strong language and explicit sexual content and is only intended for mature readers. This story may contain unconventional situations, language, and sexual encounters that may offend some readers. If you're looking for sweet, fluffy romance, I would recommend another book. This book is for mature readers (18+).

Introduction

Grab a glass of wine and get ready for a crazy, sinful, suspenseful ride. This novella continues the story of Antonio and Sabrina, along with some old friends, and new one's. I hope you enjoy!

 Are you signed up for my newsletter?

Join today and find out all the latest in new releases, contests, giveaways, sneak peeks and more.

www.chiquitadennie.com

Latest Releases

Latest Releases from Chiquita Dennie
    The Early Years-A Prequel Short Story
    Antonio and Sabrina: Struck in Love 1, 2, 3, 4, 5
    Heart of Stone, Book 1 (Emery & Jackson)
    Heart Of Stone Book 1.5 Emery &Jackson A Valentine's Day Short
    Janice and Carlo: Captivated By His Love
    Heart of Stone, Book 2 (Jordan and Damon)
    Temptation
    Heart of Stone, Book 3 (Angela and Brent)
    Cocky Catcher
    Bossy Billionaire
    Bottoms Up Heart of Stone, Book 3.5 (Jessica and Joseph Short
    Love Shorts: A Collection of Short Stories
    Joaquin Fuertes (The Fuertes Cartel Book 1)
    Exposed (Salvation Society Novel)
    Joaquin Fuertes (The Fuertes Cartel Book 2)
    Refuel (A Driven World Novel)
    Pressure (A Driven World Novel)

Latest Releases

Until Serena (HEA World Novel)
Antonio and Sabrina: Struck in Love 5
Heart of Stone, Book 4 (Jessica and Joseph)
She's All I Need
Red Light District (A Fantasy Romance Short)
Something Gaine(Romantic Comedy)
Upcoming Releases (2022/2023):
Aydin-TN Security Book 1
Dare To Love
The Carrington Cartel Book 1
Something Earned (A Romantic Comedy)
The Carrington Cartel Book 2

Synopsis

Being the boss isn't all fun and games…

Sabrina:

After the loss that I've experienced, I can't help but pull away from Antonio.

He knows that I'm grieving and that I need time to heal.

I thought that was what I wanted anyway, but the more time that we spend apart, the more the distance between us seems to grow.

Now I'm not sure that I'll be able to find my way back to him.

Or if I even want to.

Antonio:

I've waited my whole life to sit at the helm of the De Luca Cartel.

I didn't think that it would happen like this though.

Now I'm struggling to settle into my new role and take care of my family.

My girl is in pain and pulling away from me.

I don't know how to fix it either but I'm going to need to figure it out fast if I want to keep my Sabrina.

Synopsis

Can Antonio solidify his place in this unpredictable world and keep his family safe from harm, or will the constant threats from enemies finally be too much for him?

Chapter One

Antonio

"*Arghhh!!! Running headlong toward the screams, I charged into the warehouse with Carlo, Bruno, and my team following right behind me, shooting anyone that didn't belong to the De Luca Cartel.*

We hit two guards standing at the large, stone rustic door as we push through the heavy, rough-hewn door. There's nothing but the stench of death and blood and the sight that greets me is my worst nightmare come to life: Sabrina, in a chair hunched over with blood dripping down her face, her hands tied behind her back. I try to run toward her as Carlo and Bruno hold me back.

"Let me go! She needs me." I shout, shoving them both off me. I run, falling to my knees in front of her as I check her pulse. I can't feel her heartbeat, lifting her shirt I check for bullet wounds, noticing her shallow breathing. Seeing the bruises on her face and taking in her ripped clothes, it enrages me that someone had the audacity to think they could touch her. Many people will fall to their knees and beg me for mercy before I cut their heads off. She's never

supposed to be in harm's way and they've done the one thing I swore would never happen. I yell for Carlo to help me get her out of these ropes. "Carlo, I need you to find something to help me get her out of here!" *Taking extra precaution to not cause any more damage. Hearing her low moans and whispers to protect our children.*

He stations our men at every corner to monitor if anyone attempts to enter or leave the premises and rushes over. I take the knife he holds out and I slice through the ropes, pulling her to my chest.

"Baby, wake up. Please, Bella. I need you."

Still not getting a response, I pick her up and start to carry her toward our car. Carlo holds me back and checks to make sure our men are stationed at each exit route.

"We need to get her to a doctor as soon as possible. She's bleeding all over, I can't tell where the bullet entered we have to be careful with moving her."

"Sabrina needs you to stay calm, Antonio. We all know she's strong. She'll get through this," Carlo says as we walk out and a hail of gunfire rains down upon us. We drop to the ground taking cover behind the side building as our men open fire.

"Where's Sonny?" I ask. "Get him to pull the car around to this side with Bruno."

He pulls the burner phone out and sends a message. Two minutes later, Sonny pulls around the side of the building as more gunfire and explosives are set off.

Carlo looks at me, and we have a silent conversation. I'm going to make a run for the car with Sabrina, and he's going to cover me. We've done this routine enough times to know our roles. One of us is always going to save the other.

"Don't take your eyes off Bruno. Make sure you both meet me in thirty minutes or I'm sending more men out here. I

need to get her to the hospital," I say as I stand up with Sabrina in my arms caressing and kissing her cheek.

"Brother, you can never get rid of me. Now hurry up, we don't have much time before Bruno sets off the grenades," Carlo says as he hugs me and kisses Sabrina's forehead before spinning around and shooting an enemy of ours that had breeched the alleyway.

I jump into the car, Sabrina in my arms, and Sonny speeds off in our bulletproof SUV as more bullets are sent hurtling toward our vehicle. Explosives light up the night sky behind us. My brothers will be okay. They'll make it. They have to. I bend down and kiss Sabrina's forehead, taking off my jacket and wrap it around her to keep her warm. She's lot so much blood. I send another message to our medical team to make sure the room is set up at our house. Usually, we could go to the hospital, but not knowing who Ademaro has in his pocket, I'd rather be safe and have our people cover Bella's care.

We run every red light and back road and a drive that would normally be forty-five minutes or more was miraculously only twenty. Being in Italy this summer was supposed to be a renewal for us. Five years ago, after we went through that bullshit with Alex and Camilla and the Russians, we decided to move and upgrade with more security and more guards at my Club, her job, and the kids' school in New York and Italy since we split our time between both locations and we wanted to raise the kids without all the extra tension.

I see now that drama is going to find us no matter what continent we live on.

We pull around to the back of the house to avoid the chance of the kids seeing their mom like this. I refuse to let anyone carry her into the house. We take the elevator up to our bedroom, it was the longest thirty seconds of my life. The *doctors and nurses start working immediately, kicking everyone out as I place her on the bed. I lean down to kiss her lips one last time and send a prayer up to God. I step back, and the doctor does his job, I tell him to do whatever he needs to do to get Bella back to me.*

Chapter Two

Present

"Antonio, Antonio wake up baby," Sabrina says as she nudges me from my nightmare, sweat drenching my tangled sheets, my blankets wrapped in my fists. I lie there and suck in ragged breaths; Bella moves her hand across my chest. I grip it lightly and pull her into my arms. Planting a gentle kiss on her forehead trying to slow my heart rate until I drift back to sleep. The nightmares have been off and on for the last few months. I had a feeling something or someone was coming for my family and me, and the enemy was close. I woke four hours later to an empty bed and the smell of breakfast cooking downstairs. Peals of laughter reach me from the stairwell.

I get up tossing the covers back, looking over our new bedspread Sabrina recently bought, wash my face and handle my morning routine. I need to meet with Carlo to go over plans to open another club in Italy and Japan. While I loved our New York based clubs we needed to continue expanding and growing.

I turn off the shower and head to my closet when I notice Sabrina has laid out a black Armani suit for me. She always says the first thing that attracted her to me was the fit of my black suit, and my strong muscles.

Walking into the kitchen, I see Jonathan feeding Isabella a piece of bacon and AJ doing some homework at the counter. He's always waiting until the very last minute to do his schoolwork, reminding me so much of myself when I was his age. Sometimes I have to remind myself to watch what I say and do, because he watches and mimics every gesture. Sabrina spoils all of our kids rotten, especially AJ. I can't blame her though since it was just the two of them against the world thanks to that asshole Alex.

"Morning, Babe. Your food's still warm. Have a seat and I'll get you a cup of coffee." Sabrina kisses me on the lips and motions for me to sit next to Isabella.

Tickling my little princess and ruffling Jonathan's hair, I kiss all three of my kids and help Isabella with her breakfast.

"What do you have planned for today, Bella?"

With her back turned to me, I can see the outline of the thong she's wearing through her skirt. She's playing a dangerous game trying to get out of the house in that outfit. Her hair's down, styled in big waves with minimal makeup just like I like it.

"I'm meeting with Janice after I drop AJ off at school and then I'm heading in to work. I have a big meeting today," she says as she sets my plate of toast, scrambled eggs, and fruit in front of me and turns away. I grab her wrist to stop her and lean up out of my seat for a kiss.

"Who do you have the meeting with?"

"What's with the twenty questions, Tony?" she responds snarkily and wipes Jonathan's hands free of syrup and juice.

"Just making sure my wife is protected, that's all."

She rolls her eyes and leans over to feed Jonathan some more food. I look over the homework AJ was working on.

"AJ, what are you working on buddy?"

He shrugs his shoulders and I give it back to him. Sabrina sips on her morning tea as she watches over our children. It's almost 7:45 am. Time for me to head out for my meeting.

I rinse my plate and place it in the sink and kiss the kids, coming around to Sabrina last. "Sonny is driving you around today. Make sure you text me when you leave the office. Are the kids going to be with Catherine at daycare?"

"Yes, just like they've always been Antonio. I'm not the same innocent woman you met at Ryde all those years ago. I can take care of myself, you know, sometimes I feel smothered with all the security," she says and goes around the table, grabbing all the plates from the kids.

I pull her into my arms and place a hand under her chin, lifting her head.

"You're my heart, Bella, I refuse to go through what happened all those years ago again. I understand living with the constant protection is tough, but with everything that's happened in the past and my role being more demanding in the public eye. Plus the media won't let up with me being married to you as the CEO of major Financial Corporation, it would make me feel better if you didn't give the guys a hard time."

I watch her big brown eyes stare back at me understandingly. We meet halfway in a kiss as all the kids clap in excitement at us playing around. Rubbing up and down her shoulder, I move down to squeeze her perfect ass and left out with one more kiss on her lips.

"'Tonight, I'm taking you out. Have Janice bring her two rug rats over for a sleepover."

Laughing, she reaches up and deepens the kiss.

"Yes, Mr. De Luca." She murmured.

Chapter Three

Antonio

Arriving at my office, I parked in my designated space, leaving my keys with the valet. I walk into my office building and head to my floor. I send a text to Sabrina to remind her to stick with Sonny throughout the day and not to run off with her girls. I bump into my new assistant, Salina Moretti. She's been with me for over two months now and I've still been too nervous to tell Sabrina about her. She's said many times in our relationship that *I'm* the jealous and possessive one. Well, any woman so much as looks my way and *she's* ready to put them six feet under.

"Mr. De Luca, I have all of your messages. And Carlo is waiting for you in his office." Salina informs and follows me inside, taking my trench coat off and hanging it up by the door. She leans over sexily in front of us both, pouring Carlo and I a cup of coffee and sets it at the desk before passing me the messages and leaving the room, shutting the door behind her.

"She's going to be a problem," Carlo suggested and takes a sip from his cup.

"I'm a happily married man, and she has a boyfriend." I respond placing the cup down on the desk.

"Mark my words Antonio, as soon as Sabrina or Janice find out you have your own personal version of Beyonce working in your office, you're gonna be in for nothing but hell. Remember, don't come running to my house to find someone to talk some sense into your wife. We both know she can get crazy with her hands."

I wave off his comment and reach for the file across my desk with the information on Ademaro Guerrero.

"Did you have another dream?" Carlo asks.

"Yeah, I know something's coming our way, but I just can't figure out what it is. Things are too calm and I've heard whispers that this new Prime Minister is trying to encroach on our territory."

"Based on what I've heard from my contacts, after Sabrina helped to cover up your involvement with Camilla's death and you gave her brother Angelo the casino percentage and local territory in the Bronx, that didn't buy us as much good will as we thought it would. We might have made a mistake with breaking up those areas. Italy is the backbone of our operation and that affects everything that happens in America. Unfortunately, it's not helping matters any to have your father going behind your back and working with the enemy," Carlo responded as he pulled out his vibrating phone and answered the call.

He looked annoyed with whoever's on the other end.

He finally hangs up, running a hand down his face, trying to compose himself.

"We need to contact Bruno and the other Capos in Italy. That was my source in the Guerrero Family. They want to plan a meeting with the Capos to try and lure them over to their side."

I slap my hand down on the table.

"What the fuck!" Salina busts through the door. "Sir, are you alright. I heard a loud noise?" Salina asks rushing to grasp my hand.

I motion for her to close the door and leave me. "I'm fine Salina. Can you reschedule my meetings for the rest of the day and I'll call my wife about our dinner plans at the restaurant?"

Salina nods and walks back out of the room without responding.

"Has anyone contacted my father yet?"

"Bruno reached out and spoke with your mother. You know his retirement wouldn't last long and he despises traveling around together. She was more stressed from him still keeping in touch with his brother's contacts. She said he's traveling to Spain and will probably head to Italy if his business gets finished early," Carlo states as he fires another text message off.

"You know what we have to do right?" I ask. "We have to bring Angelo in on this, since he controls a piece of the land that brings in all our undercover arms sales. If Ademaro Guerrero gets a hold of Angelo's territory and has the vote of all the Capos behind him, we'll have World War III on our hands."

* * *

The next day we leave our cars at the private runway and arrive in Japan. "My Love, make sure you stick with your security while I'm away and keep Janice close. I shouldn't be gone long baby, and give the kids a kiss and hug for me."

I leave a voice message as we pull up at Ryde, our newest club in Japan. Carlo and I walk in as our men follow behind. The crew are cleaning and setting up for the night.

"What do you have for me, Sonny? I need all the information you have on Angelo Ricci and Ademaro," I ask as we head to my office in the back.

During this time the club was closed to the public, besides the normal deliveries, cleaning crews, and those preparing for the night crowd. Our clubs all run the same. This one is as lively as the Italian Ryde, and even sexier. Only we have more Cartel members hanging around Japan. The good thing is that a truce is set up in the area and no killing is the law around here. Sabrina and the girls like to get out every blue moon and they chose Ryde as the destination whenever we are in this part of the world. Priority is always to check each person that enters or exits.

On the way to my office, the manager of the club stops me. "What's going on, Fernando?" I questioned, feeling my phone vibrating in my pocket.

"Mr. De. Luca, the liquor company shorted us three cases of Belvedere, something about getting stopped from delivering without permission." I nodded, annoyed that the Yakuza could potentially be meddling in our affairs. Brining on another crime family in the mix would hinder my potential negotiations with our current families in the US and Italy.

Keeping my composure and not allowing my annoyance to show in front of my men, I took the paperwork from him as I headed into the office.

"How many more clubs are you planning to open?" Sonny asked.

"As many as I want. Now tell me what's going with my father," I demand while looking over the liquor contract with the distributor.

"He has somehow gotten it in his head that your time as Capo hasn't benefitted the family. You've gone soft since being with Sabrina, and having kids. Enemies are coming from all directions, and you lack what the De Luca Cartel needs to control all of the European territory. He wants to go global with the Cartel," Sonny informs me as he passes photos of my father and Ademaro talking in front of what appears to be government buildings in Italy.

"Interesting turn of events, we have someone following your father. They've reported that he's taking meetings with some high profile bosses in Spain, my contact mentioned seeing him with a woman?"

Carlo shakes his head at the photos given to him.

"Your mom's not doing so well. I wanted to tell you earlier, but she swore me to secrecy."

"Tomorrow we'll fly out to get her. She'll put up a fight, but with Dad acting without the Cartel's permission, I need to keep her close. I find it funny how he hasn't forgiven me for killing his brother, the person that was involved with Sabrina's kidnapping. Alfredo wanted to take over everything, kill me, and yet our father thinks me getting married to Sabrina is a distraction. I've never been more clear and focused on my future and the Cartel's since her kidnapping."

My family is slowly slipping away from me the deeper I get involved in the business that I promised my wife and mother I'd let my brother and Carlo run. Lately, my nightmares have become more apparent to those around me and my motives have become more transparent. Ademaro is an enemy I need to put to rest before he grows stronger. Once we find out if Angelo Ricci is helping him or my father, I can't promise that a double funeral won't be set in motion.

I pick up the office phone and dialing my father's number. After two rings he answers. I placed him on speakerphone, trying to gather my thoughts before I explode.

"Didn't think it would take you this long son," he says with a hint of arrogance in his voice.

"I didn't either. Seems you've been a very busy man." I lean closer to the phone making sure to listen for any background noise that may give away his location.

"How is your wife?" he questions.

"Leave her out of this," I snap in response, shoving up from the chair, and crossing my arms over my chest.

"Why? This all started with her, might as well end with her."

Hearing those words and then the sound of a dial tone lets me know he hung up on me. I close my eyes, trying to gather my thoughts and not blow up.

"Argghhh!" I yell and fling everything from my desk to the floor.

***

Two days later.

"Why do you seem so distracted, Antonio?" Sabrina pouted, sitting across from me at our favorite restaurant. "You promised there would be no thinking about work. You said you'd leave your phone off while the kids stayed with Janice and Carlo tonight." Lately I've been staying up late at night in my office, coming to bed after two and three in the morning. Carlo and Bruno are coming around more often and whenever Sabrina came into the room things would get quiet. Something was happening and I needed to prepare.

We used to have regular date nights in the beginning of our marriage. We traveled back and forth between America and Italy a lot finally deciding to buy a house stateside to raise our kids. I wanted her to feel safe, untouched from my lifestyle, to show her how I grew up. Over the past few weeks, my busy schedule has kept me away from home far too often. The kids are getting bigger and needing more of her attention. Opening the clubs across the world are forcing me to travel more often and farther away from home. Taking advice from Carlo I planned on focusing more on us with taking her on a trip, just the two of us away from the kids, her work, and the dealings with my family business.

I reach out for her hand and I kiss her wedding ring, reminding myself just how lucky I'd become with making Bella my one and only.

"Do you remember the many times you brushed me off and I had to beg you to go out on a date with me?" I joked as she smirked.

She bites the corner of her bottom lip.

She looks beautiful tonight and I have plans to keep her up all night with my tongue between her legs. Lately she's shied away from sex and I know it's because of the miscarriage. I wish Sabrina would realize that we both lost a child together, and keeping that distance wouldn't help her to heal any faster. Being close like we used to be, and sharing that connection, along with spending more time with our kids and friends, would help us to move on.

Chapter Four

S**abrina**

He quickly changes the subject as always. But knowing him, he wouldn't straight out tell me what's going on even if I asked him point blank. I know deep down it's mafia business or something to do with his father, though. Picking up the glass of water, I take a sip, placing the glass down staring into his eyes.

"I have to fly out tomorrow," Antonio said, tightening his grip on my hand as I tried to jerk it away.

"Okay," I dryly answered.

His gaze spelled he wasn't happy with my answer, but tough shit. I'm not the naive woman he met in the club that night. I'm fully aware of what the business is on both the legal and illegal fronts.

"Bella, don't act like that. I'm going to bring my mother back here and check on our home."

"I didn't say anything, Antonio. You have this all planned out apparently. I'll keep my mouth shut. Can we go? I'm no longer hungry or in the mood for this," I answer removing the napkin from my lap, flinging it down on the table and abruptly standing up.

His eyes narrow into dark slits as a cold shiver runs down my spine. He motions for the waitress to come over. I just want to get out of here and head home to my babies.

"Are you ready to order sir?" the waitress asks as I start to stand up and leave.

"Yes. Sabrina, sit down," Antonio started. His voice was harsh, with an edge.

I jerked back at his icy tone and peered deep into his eyes. Trying to find any trace of where the man that used to stay up late with me in the middle of the night and pigged out on snacks, or watched cheesy reality TV shows, or took me on surprise dates just the two of us had disappeared to. We had a stare off as the waitress stood still, not knowing what to do.

"Can you give us a minute, please?" I told, sitting back down and clasping my hands together, leaning over the table.

"If you ever speak to me with that tone again, Antonio, we're going to have a problem. I suggest you remember whom you are talking to. This is a fifty-fifty marriage. I'm not your mother or any of the women you've dated before, and you will not speak to me in that way." I call for the waitress to come back over as I stare daggers into his eyes. Antonio tilted his head at an angle and smiled.

"I'd like to order a large pan of lasagna to go, two loaves of garlic bread, two bottles of wine, and the most expensive dessert you have on the menu and charge it to his card."

"Sit down Bella," Antonio snidely says.

"Uhmm..." the waitress says, not knowing who to take direction from.

"I'll wait in the car while you pay for dinner. Oh, and

Happy Anniversary, honey." I reply, striding out of the restaurant with Sonny and the other bodyguards hot on my heels.

* * *

A few minutes later the car door opens, and Antonio slides inside. Out of the corner of my eye I feel his hard glare on me. I sit over in the corner of the limousine as far away from him as I can get, as the driver pulls off.

"Sorry, Baby." He finally sighs and rubs his hands down his face.

"Fuck you and the..."

Before I can get the rest of my sentence out, he pulls me against his stiff muscles. "I would like that very much Bella," he says, his eyes fixed upon my lips.

"Antonio, you forgot our anniversary," I tell him, shoving against his chest so I could look into his eyes. "This is serious. I'm not playing."

His lips curve up in amusement and I roll my eyes as he moves his hands under my dress. I slap his hand away. He buries his face in my neck, trailing kisses down my jawline.

"Please, Baby, forgive me. Let me make it up to you. I'll never speak that way to you again, Sabrina... Bella." He threads his fingers through my loose curls.

"Stop." I say, my dark brows tangling in a scowl. "You don't get to seduce me into forgiving your behavior tonight. I want time together without you taking off for weeks at a time." It's not too much to ask. I know it's not.

He lays a hand on my thigh, and my heartbeat quickens as we stop abruptly, tires screeching. The driver rolls the divider down as Antonio pulls me close behind him, his hand hovering over his holstered gun.

"Sir, we have a road block up ahead, do you want to detour or stick to this route?" Salvatore asked.

Antonio fuming pulls his cell phone out of his pocket to text someone, I assume it's either Sonny or Carlo. Seeing his nostrils flared, and the anger flashing across his face reminded me of that time I called myself breaking up with him after one night. Reminiscing of that time. I wasn't planning on getting involved with another man and he'd showed up at my office making me feel things I never wanted to feel. His eyes bore into me and tugged at emotions I thought I put on ice after my last relationship and dealing with cheating from Alex. Letting my heart open to him not knowing the possibilities of what I would have given up with having our three kids.

"Do you think this is a legit roadblock or something else?" I question as he taps away on his phone, ignoring my question.

His fingers grip my wrist suddenly and he looks deep into my eyes. "I need you to trust me, Bella. The day we met, you became mine. And I'll do anything to keep you safe. Everything is going to be okay." He draws me into his arms kissing me on the forehead.

Hearing those words, I feel a sense of calm wash over my body. I know he loves me and I know he will stop at nothing to keep me and our family safe. But, as our lives have gotten deeper in the Cartel. I see him less and less as the man I fell in love with.

My door is suddenly torn open, and I cling to Antonio's hold. I won't be kidnapped again.

"Baby's it's just Sonny...shush ...it's okay."

I relax and for a moment, I wondered whether this would lead to another year of us being separated. I loosen my arms from around his neck and we both step out of the limousine.

"Our contact says this is Angelo's doing. He's

summoned you to meet with him now. He'd had someone watching Sabrina and figured once you two left dinner you'd be in a more agreeable mood to discuss business," Sonny says, enraged at the situation.

"He must've forgotten that I don't play by his rules. Get all of this bullshit moved and take Sabrina home. I'll deal with him once my wife gets home safe," Antonio hisses, venom dripping from every word.

"Baby, come home with me," I plead with him. "Please. I don't like the way this looks. Angelo is probably setting you up," I whisper, unease creeping into my voice. "You told me you wouldn't keep doing this."

"Go with Sonny, and I promise to wake you when I get home." He says, his hands resting lower on my back, keeping me close in his arms. My skin grows hot as his warm breath feathers against my cheek.

This could be the last time he hugs me.

"Don't get upset and start a war," I tell him, pissed.

"Mmm. I can't promise that Mi Amore..."

I step out of his embrace.

"You promised no killing, did you forget about my kidnapping, or the fire a few years back?" I remind him crossing my arms over my chest. I can't believe I have to remind him. "Letting Carlo handle the heavier load should be your only decision, Tony." I sigh. I'm a mix of mad and frustrated. I'm so disappointed looking at my husband right now, seeing a little grey hair, and lines in his brow that appear whenever he gets upset. Taking on this responsibility has matured him some ways, and other ways made him appear older than he was.

"I can promise that I'll be home before the kids go off to school."

"Fine, just don't think I'll be there." I mumble.

"What was that?" Antonio questions, closing the space between us and wrapping both of his hands around my waist. He bends down to kiss my lips, and I let him without hesitation. This man is my everything, but his stubbornness to always be in control and running the Cartel seems to be his only priority these days.

Chapter Five

A**ntonio**
I tapped her on the hip to head toward Sonny's car as I got back into the limo and told the driver to keep driving while sending a text to Carlo to meet at Angelo's location.

Carlo: *Where's Sabrina?*

Me: *She's with Sonny heading home. Have a car trail them and keep extra protection on the kids once she picks them up.*

Carlo: *Is that a good idea to wake them up this late?*

Me: *Knowing Sabrina she'll want them close to her tonight. Make sure you have protection on Janice.*

Carlo: *Don't worry about that, soon as my phone vibrated she jumped up grabbing Betsy, ready for anything.*

I laugh at his comment, picturing Janice sleeping with a gun under her pillow, ready for the moment someone says anything about messing with her family or friends. Once old trusted Betsy comes out, there's no turning back.

The car pulls up to a dark alleyway and we're assaulted

with the stench of death, booze, and pussy. To the outsider it's an average looking old building with homeless people hanging around. Once you step inside you're met with booze, liquor, strippers, gambling, drugs, and anything else illegal you might want to get your hands on. Angelo could make it happen here. I only allow him to keep this place running out of respect for the history of our families' dealings. But after tonight, I can't promise that I'd still feel generous about letting him live, much less staying in business. The homeless were the lookouts, but we had the cops, mayor, and governor in our pockets. So I wasn't worried about anyone ratting us out. Being married to Sabrina, I have to be more aware of how I'm perceived to the outside world, as my wife is very prominent in the public eye.

Stepping out of the limo, I see Carlo and Bruno pull up at the same time with more bodyguards. Angelo Ricci doesn't scare me, so Carlo coming with backup is the least of my worries.

"Did she get the kids?" I inquire, checking my gun in the holster as I button up my suit jacket.

"Yeah, and I'm going to get dragged into your bullshit of you forgetting your anniversary. Janice will kick me out of the house because she thinks I have some sort of influence over you and you keep fucking up. Your wife complained and now I'm stuck not getting any pussy for a week," Carlo complains, groaning and rolling his eyes.

A worried look crosses his face, and I want to laugh at his predicament, when all of a sudden a door opens and a herd of rodents scurry by. Trash lingers in the hallway we step into and the door slams shut behind us.

"Boss says you need to leave your guns in the car," Angelo's goon spits the words out through gritted teeth, clearly pissed at our sudden arrival.

Smiling at his suggestion, a flash of movement catches my eye as Bruno lunges and cocks his gun, breaking his jaw as my men take him outside to try and reach an amicable understanding.

***

I barge into Angelo's office with Carlo and Bruno behind me. Some redhead is on her knees, giving him head.

"What the fuck?" Angelo screams as Bruno pulls her off his dick before he could finish. Angelo tries to reach under his desk for a weapon, but my men and I came prepared. He shifts in his seat, holding his hands up in a pose of surrender.

Chuckling to myself, I step in closer, motioning if I could take a seat in front of his desk. He nods okay and I place my feet on top of his desk as though it was mine.

"Angelo. You're a hard man to find." I state, clasping my hands together.

"What the fuck do you want Tony? I'm tapped out. You've taken everything including my sister, businesses, and territory," Angelo responds, the myriad of emotions flitting across his face. Everything from fear of the unknown, to trying to put on a brave face and wait to see which direction this sit-down was heading in.

I'm not that heartless. His mother is still alive. "I hear you're making a lot of noise behind my back Angelo. Didn't we have an understanding that I allow you to live and run this shit hole of a casino without any interference as long as we get a cut?"

Fear clogged his throat, I saw him attempting to reach for his gun, Bruno pressed his pistol underneath his chin. I dismissed him with a wave to lower his gun and to give us a minute alone. Angelo's a lot of things, but stupid isn't one of them. Shooting me would be about the stupidest decision he could ever make.

"You're lucky my brother is nicer than me," I say, smirking as a text comes through from Sabrina that she's arrived home safe. Not taking the time to reply back, I place it back into my pocket and stare unflinchingly into Angelo's eyes. His wavering gaze toward the door gives me a second of hesitation.

"Is there anything you need to tell me, Angelo? I thought we made it clear about the territory and who runs things."

"I still find it hard to believe you think I had anything to do with some of your property getting confiscated by the police. Don't you have them on your payroll?"

"I'm here about Ademaro in Italy, running for Prime Minister and what he's after. The confiscation will be dealt with momentarily. Do I need to remind you who I am? Camilla betrayed me and look where she ended up."

He tried to jump up and reach for me, but my reflexes are still lightning quick. I pull my gun out of my holster and shoot, hitting him in the forearm.

"Agghhh! You bastard." Angelo hollered falling back in his seat, blood covering his hands and shirt.

"Now you have about five minutes before you bleed out and die, or I can get my men to get you some help. All I need you to do is find out what he's is doing in Italy. We can be friends Angelo, or enemies, the decision is yours," I say, standing and wiping my gun off with a monogramed handkerchief that Sabrina bought for a father's day gift a few years ago.

"Fuck... shit...alright."

"Don't try and talk, save your breath. You'll need it, my

men will help you and I'll have Bruno get you to a doctor," I tell him, walking toward the door, pausing at his final words.

"Ademaro is an enemy you shouldn't go up against. Especially if you've dealt with tragedy in the past," Angelo admitted.

I turn, looking over my shoulder as Bruno and our security detail walk inside with the doctor on call.

"You're a witness," I tell Angelo. "Whenever someone makes an enemy of Antonio De Luca, they always find themselves on the other side of my gun. Oh, by the way, how's your mother doing?" I taunt, turning back around and going back toward my car with Carlo following behind.

"You going after his mother?" Carlo asked.

I signal my driver off from holding the door open and step inside followed by Carlo as I mull over Angelo's words about my handling of a new enemy.

"Find out as much as you can on Ademaro. The dream I had was real in some way. I've felt like something was brewing for a while and expected after we fully stepped into more legit businesses, that our rivals would try and take over our territory."

"I'll have something for you in the morning. Go home and sleep for now. Especially if we're going to get your mother tomorrow." Carlo says as he types away on his phone. Watching the smile on his face, I figured Janice was texting him about something that wasn't work related. Sabrina has me looking the same way whenever she sends photos of herself, taunting me to come home fast.

I lean my head back, closing my eyes. I have to figure out a way to get rid of another snake in the well before they come for my family or me.

Chapter Six

Sabrina
I couldn't sleep at all last night. I got up super early to get the kids ready for school and avoid Antonio. Our differences in opinion on his actions with this situation will only bring more drama upon us that we don't need. Putting my family further in the spotlight is something we cannot afford.

"Does he know you're here?" Janice shouts over the metal wall of the barrier that separates us.

This is our weekly shooting practice. I need something to keep my mind off not only our anniversary being forgotten and ruined, but also Antonio getting even deeper in the family business. He'd promised to allow Carlo or Bruno to handle things since they took over as the face of the family. But the power that comes with the Cartel is a drug he never really quit. He only hid it from us. Now I'm becoming even more entrenched in his business as his wife, or Donna as they call me at the annual dinners with the other wives. Recalling our past moments with spending our anniversary together away from the kids and our businesses.

We'd fly away to a secluded island and enjoy a week together without any drama. Well, we would still have security around us, but they stayed in a separate area so our privacy was still assured.

I reload and check the nine-millimeter and raise my arms locked in on my target and fire off a round. "Nope. He came home late and I wasn't in bed."

"What? Where did you sleep?" Janice asks quizzically, stepping out of her section.

"I slept in AJ's room. He doesn't like to fight in front of the kids, so I slept with my baby to avoid him. Plus, I knew he'd want sex and I wasn't in the mood. Our entire night was ruined on top of him forgetting our anniversary." I set off another shot, pissed at Antonio all over again.

"Maybe you're overreacting Sabrina. I mean, I wasn't the biggest fan of Antonio in the beginning. But he's grown on me. I don't think he's trying to intentionally hurt you."

"Uhmm, Janice this isn't about you."

"Yeah, but what did you expect when you married a mobster? Sunshine and rainbows? Cookies and fishing on a farm? I mean…"

"I get your point."

"Do you? Because you're sounding real selfish right now. That man has been through a lot, not only from being forced to distance himself with his family, getting shot, but also losing a year away from his child."

"Are you married to Antonio or am I?" I wonder, putting the gun down and pushing the side call button to bring the sheet forward.

She rolls her eyes at me and I chortle, shaking my head. I take the sheet down. Three shots burned through the paper hitting the target's shoulder, head, and chest.

"Someone was getting some aggression out today. Look

at your hits; head chest and shoulder. He must've taught you well to always go for the jugular." Janice replies.

"Have you spoken with Liz today? I know she's almost in the final stretch of her pregnancy?" I asked, abruptly changing the subject not wanting to deal with my tumultuous emotions about my marriage.

"Slick with the subject change missy. But yes, I spoke with her a few days ago. She's getting bigger and bigger everyday. Baby is kicking her butt and Bruno is not letting her do anything but sleep and eat."

"You know how he gets when it comes to Liz, he's more obsessed than Antonio is with me." I respond handing over my gun and leftover ammo to the clerk.

"That's true, I didn't think a man alive could be more into his wife more than Antonio and Carlo, but Bruno has proven me wrong."

I flicked my tongue out, nudged her in the arm for dissing my man as we waved goodbye.

We make our way to the exit to head out. I canceled my clients for today except for one conference call that I can take care of from home. With three kids, my priorities have shifted to focus more on them and Antonio.

Janice opens the driver's side door as I slide into the passenger side. I get my phone out. I need to call my sister and make plans for dinner we haven't spent any time together in a while, since our lives have gotten busier and me being a wife and mother. I wanted her to know she's just as important to me.

"What a nice surprise it is to hear from you Sabrina Washington. Oops. I meant Sabrina De Luca." Ashley giggles over the phone.

"Ha ha, very funny. What are you doing?" I ask. I'm exhausted already and it's only 11 am.

"Nothing. Just at the hospital. Trying to figure out when I can visit you and the kids. Mom and Dad have been bugging me to transfer to a hospital near them again. They think it will be better for after they retire. " Ashley explains.

"That reminds me, I need to plan a retirement party for them."

"Still can't believe Pops is leaving you the company. Are you prepared for the change in workload being the CEO of a large company that needs your undivided attention is going to do to your life?" Ashley asks, making me nervous all over again. I haven't even talked to Antonio about my new role yet. I doubt he'd understand me being away for work. I just feel like I need this. I don't want to be away from the kids, but I've been so lonely. Antonio is never around so it's just easier to be in work mode. Especially after the miscarriage, it just feels like we are two trains passing in the night sometimes.

"When did you decide this Sabrina?" Janice's eavesdropping ass asks.

Now I have to tell Antonio. Janice doesn't keep anything from Carlo.

"So, who are you seeing lately Ashley?"

Out the corner of my eye I can see Janice glaring at me with a deep scowl on her face.

"Please tell me Antonio knows about this?" Ashley says.

I groaned in annoyance. It's like everybody has an opinion about my marriage now. We promised to not keep things from each other and here I am taking this job at my family's company that will keep me away from my own family.

And here I am mad at him for doing the same damn thing.

"Can we talk about this another day?" I ask, feeling a

headache coming on from all the endless stress. "Actually, Janice, can we have lunch another time? I'm still tired from last night."

"Sabrina you know how..."

I cut her off and we stare silently at each other as Ashley tries drawing my attention back to her and I just abruptly end the call.

***

Seeing no cars parked outside the house, I figure Antonio is at the club attending to business.

I jog upstairs to our bedroom and throw my purse on the floor. Taking my shirt, and sweats off, I walk toward the bathroom and turn the water on. The kids don't get out of daycare until three so I have time to just be.

As the steam settles, I peer into the mirror, looking at my reflection, trying to see myself. What I've become. I'm not the same woman I was five years ago. I was dealing with a bad breakup then. I was gaining a name for myself as a businesswoman. I was a person that exuded confidence in whatever she set her mind to. Now I'm a mother of three kids, wife to a Mafia kingpin. Shooting and running from guns, and discussing political strategy and how it best serves the Cartel and my family's business.

And a mother who has lost a child.

I brush tears off my cheeks. My overactive imagination is in overdrive wondering what my life would look like now if I had never met Antonio. I wouldn't have these beautiful children, but I would have more of me left inside. More of me looking back in the mirror.

I step into the shower and wash away the morning and

the tears. I'll call and apologize to the girls when I pull myself together.

Fifteen minutes later I step out of the shower, grabbing a towel and lotion on the way out to the bedroom.

"Did you have fun?" Antonio says quietly from the bed and I nearly jump out of my skin.

Chapter Seven

Antonio

"What are you doing here?" She asks stepping further into the room and sitting down on her new cream reading couch. She saw it and, on a whim, bought it for herself so she'd be able to read her romance novels. All night long she was talking about this one from this author that writes short erotic romance stories, I think it was called "*Wet Heat.*" I love that she reads. I love that she knows what she wants and takes it unapologetically. I don't think she knows how much I love her. And maybe I haven't shown her enough. Many people view men like me as arrogant, possessive, and hard all the time, but the one thing that brings me to my knees is my family. Not being able to protect her from losing the baby and not knowing if I caused the miscarriage will stay with me for the rest of my life. Deep down, I feel this overwhelming guilt everyday, grieving over what our child would have looked like or what they would have become. She's right in the sense I don't express my emotions a lot and that comes with the way I grew up, we weren't taught to display our emotions in a healthy way. Probably why I tend to shut off my emotions and kill so easily.

I take my jacket off and lay it over the chair before coming closer to her. "I'm sorry about our anniversary dinner. I've been a fool. Can you forgive me?" I hold my arms out for her, hoping that she'll walk into them.

She lowers her head and walks into my embrace, holding her towel tight.

"Did you have fun at the gun range?" I tilt her head up, gazing into her eyes.

She rolls her eyes and smacks my hand away and sits on the edge of the bed to put her lotion on.

I squat down in front of her, rubbing her smooth wet thighs, as she smirks, fighting to keep her towel around her body.

"About the other night, I really am sorry. I apologize Sabrina, as your husband I never want you to feel like you're my last priority, Baby."

Her breathing increases as my hand drifts further up her legs, across her stomach, brushing past her sweet pussy that holds a little stubble of hair. I don't care if she had hair down there or not at the end of the day. I'm a well-fed man and satisfied.

I open her legs wider and lean her back further.

"Is this your way of apologizing? Because if so, I suggest you do more than eat my pussy Antonio." Sabrina whispers through a moan as my tongue swipes across her mound, already wet and ready for me. I guide her hand on top of my head and move her legs over the top of my shoulders so she was on the edge of the bed. I teased in a finger, flicked my tongue across her bud, caressing and kissing as her breasts rose and fell under her labored breathing. I felt her shudder underneath my hold and the idea of her eagerness excited me even more as my dick got hard.

"Tony, Oh God!"

"Give it to me…Amore Mio."

I rip off her towel and shifted her to the floor, missionary position. She tries to help unbuckle my pants and I say, "Let me see you play with your pussy baby." I take off my tie, and come partway out of my pants and shoes, watching as she moves one hand up to her neck, squeezing gently as the other one massages, pinches, and plays with her core.

"Damn, you've never looked more beautiful Baby."

"I need you to kiss it and make it feel better, Tesoro Mio."

"With pleasure, Bella." I explore her taut nipples, caressing and squeezing each one, licking, biting as she trails tickling fingers up and down my naked back. "Will you give me another chance to make up for our anniversary?" I question, bringing her face towards mine, staring into her eyes deeply as I align the head of my dick with her pussy, only allowing the tip to slide in for a second. "You, don't play fair." Sabrina's touch is electrifying as an electric shock scorches through my body. Not able to hold on any longer, I push through her walls as deep as possible.

"Mhmm…"

Not wanting to come too early, I pull out and lean up, wrapping her legs around my waist. I hold both hands on her hips and slowly speed up my thrusts. I think of the weather in Italy, opening up another club, even killing Ademaro. Anything I could possibly think of to avoid cuming so soon.

"Fuck! Baby, aghhh." Sweat pours down my forehead, as we meet each other thrust for thrust.

"Right there, just like that...baby," Sabrina groans, poking her nails into my arms, tears rolling down her cheeks.

The sounds of our naked bodies colliding, and our moans, echo throughout the room reminding me that at any time Carlo or our nanny could come looking for us for anything.

"Get on top, Sabrina." I ease out slowly, kissing her lower lips, and help her straddle me reverse cowgirl, her favorite position.

Before I can say anything, she grips my dick and takes me all the way to down her throat.

"Fuck! Tesoro Mio, baby, please." I moan, right as I smack her plump ass, pulling her over my face as we give each other oral pleasure. She sucks my dick hungrily, with my dick hitting the back of her throat.

"Remember, I don't play fair, Antonio. You may be the Capo to those men out there, but I run shit in here," she taunts, squeezing my dick and fondling my balls. I ease index finger in her tight asshole, her juices glisten in the soft lighting of our bedroom, going back and forth with my tongue and one finger in her pussy as we fight for dominance over each other.

"Antonio!" she shouts as I move her down to slide her onto my throbbing dick.

We both shiver at the intrusion.

"I want to renew our vows," I whisper with a moan. Often men don't want to be heard making any noises during sex, thinking it makes them weak. But I couldn't hold back the way she made me feel. She's the one that can see my vulnerability, my love as her husband and father of her children and not the Capo of the De Luca Cartel.

* * *

As she blissfully sleeps, I slip out of her arms to shower and grab my phone. I step inside turning the water on to the highest temperature that Sabrina always hated whenever we showered together. Letting the water run over my head as my eyes close thinking of the next steps in my plan. After twenty minutes I turn the water off, stepping out and drying off. Checking my phone I notice a text from Carlo. Leaving out of the bathroom and grabbing a pair of boxers and fresh shirt and pants. I shook my head laughing quietly as Sabrina lightly snored. She argued me down that she never snores. I was tempted to record her for evidence, but changed my mind and went to my office to return Carlo's text from earlier.

"How long have you been here?" I inquired surprised by Carlo showing up, as I went around and took a seat at my desk.

"Your housekeeper let me in about ten minutes ago. She went to go get the kids and I told her I'd let you two sleep a little longer." Carlo stands and passes me a folder.

"Any difficulty with getting the information?"

"No, at the moment she's seen out with him during his campaign stops, so it works in our favor." Carlo replied.

"Nothing out of the ordinary," I mutter to myself, flipping through the surveillance photos and records of Queen Vitale.

"I think Ademaro is a puppet for Queen." Carlo stated, leaning over my desk pointing to a photo of Ademaro and Queen huddled close standing in front of a limo.

"How is she connected to him?" I inquire, picking up my phone and sending the phone records for my tech to investigate.

"Based on what Bruno found out, she has him strategically placed as the Prime Minister. She's getting everyone under her thumb to make decisions for the Cartel families. Antonio, we have to tread lightly with this situation, " Carlo explains, standing up strolling over to the wet bar and pouring a glass of water. We continue strategizing what our response might be to this new development. Two hours later, I hear a knock and the door opens. "What are you two doing?" Sabrina says, heading into my office, freshly showered and dressed from her afternoon nap.

"Bella, I have to go out of town and check on my mother, possibly bring her back here."

"How long will you be gone?" she questions, following us out of my office toward the kitchen.

"At most three days, I'm hoping just one. Depends on my mother's health."

"Are you planning on speaking with your father while you are there?" she wonders heading to open the fridge to grab a bottle of water out of its depths.

"Of course, but you don't have to stress about my family dynamics. I'll be back before the week is out. Carlo, will you call and setup the jet. Tell them we're on our way."

Carlo nods, walking out making the call as Sabrina peers at me with deep seeded anger and walks off as I try to reach and pull her into my arms.

She motions for me to give her space and I agree, sighing in frustration. Carlo comes back into the hallway as I pass him the folder and he smirks knowing I'm in trouble once again.

"Your dick won't get you out of this one."

"Fuck you." I hiss, stomping upstairs to grab my bag and leave specific instructions with the security detail.

* * *

Carlo and Sonny flew with me to check in on my mother and possibly have her fly back to the states. Trying to convince my father was a second issue I hoped to resolve, him going behind my back to secure a deal with him cutting the family out and overthrowing me as Capo. Our jet landed at our private airspace, Sonny made sure to have cars waiting with security.

"Mr. De Luca, we've arrived at our destination you can unbuckle and deplane," the flight attendant says and I thank her.

"Where's Bruno?" I question Sonny as we all step off the plane and walk toward my bulletproof town car.

"He's at your parents' house. Said to come straight there so you guys can talk." Sonny responds and I pass him my bag, watching for anything out of place around the area. Even though it's a secure airport for my family business, I still have guards stationed at every area of the hanger. No one can come in or out without going through Bruno or I. Mostly we take family trips on the jet. I haven't seen my parents in about a year. We've spoke over the phone, well my kids and I have spoke with Madre. Over the past few years my father had became someone I didn't recognize. The hatred he still harbored for the killing of his brother, my marriage to Sabrina, and me not including him in the business has pushed him too far.

We all slide inside and Sonny sits up front with the driver, giving him directions.

Chapter Eight

Queen

We're all sitting here waiting for the guest of honor to arrive so we can discuss our strategy of getting the much needed votes. We're taking over areas in Italy that sit between two Cartel families that currently have a truce. I plan to take over everything with the help of Ademaro as the political foe setting up barriers for storeowners to have to fall in line with the demands we set in place. I await updates from my enforcer in the Russian mob and keep an eye on my contacts in America. Angelo's a pussy that couldn't even avenge his sister or family's name. I have him in my pocket, based on the photos of Antonio visiting him the other night it seems like this would be the perfect time to pay a visit to my American friends.

He's onboard with lining our Cartel with names of local storeowners and officials that oversee cities in local areas. We could have the politicians and media in my hand, and eventually branch out to having the Vitale name rise to prominence in America. Antonio has no idea that I have a deal already ironed out with his father to run things, as long as I cut him in by fifteen percent, which comes to zero because the first chance I get, Don De Luca will be no longer breathing the same air as me. That son of bitch has no loyalty to his children because he married a black woman. I'm black, but my money's green so I guess we can do business. My goal is to get everyone in the local government and military in my pocket, I have photos, recordings, and names of things that could be very hurtful if made public. *What can I say? I love money, and power.* I say to myself as the door opens and Ademaro steps inside and with his assistant following along behind him obediently like a lapdog. I put on the fakest smile, to sell him this false dream.

"Queen, what are you doing here? Our meeting is later this week I thought?" He motions his assistant to give us some privacy.

I stand and smooth down my black halter dress. It's a dress that gives every man the illusion I would sell my soul to be on his arm. Only they'd be playing into my hand, and I'd give them a false sense of security until I didn't need them anymore.

I reach out for a hug, we kiss on both cheeks, and he presses his groin into my stomach. He grasps my waist, pulling me in tighter and smelling my hair, squeezing my ass. I move his hand away and lightly tap his cheek to stop. Stepping back, I lean on the edge of his desk.

"How are the discussions going? I see your numbers are rising in the polls?" I say. As the daughter of an Italian American mafia boss and his mistress, I use my smarts and assets to get what I want. Don't think I didn't grow up without my father. I'm his greatest achievement. He's always been proud of me because I'm as hard as any man would be. The only problem is that I need to be the behind the scenes of the business, because the culture still didn't accept women as Capos in Cartels. My mother, after a while, didn't want anything to do with my father because he never left his wife. She always wanted me to find love, get married, and happiness away from the dangers of Cartel life. For myself, I thrived in the lifestyle; I loved being the daughter of Federico Vitale and a mafia princess. Everyone knew our family name in Italy, and a few parts of America.

"You should let me take you out for lunch. We can discuss it over champagne," he said, lifting my chin, leaning down to peck my lips.

"Focus Ademaro. I didn't come here for lunch. I need to know that we have everyone on board with getting the De Luca Cartel under my leadership."

"You mean my leadership, right?" he replies and walks around to his desk opening his legs, tapping his thigh for me to sit.

"Don't get too self-involved, thinking you're running the show. I put you in place here and I can remove you just as quickly."

He chuckled, tapping his finger on the desk and opening a file I had placed for him to look over. It was photos of Angelo, Antonio, and his family in America. I've had my spies watching every player in the game.

"When did you get these?"

"Unlike you, I'm always focused on the task at hand. I spoke with my contact and then his father relayed that his mother wasn't feeling well. So, he's coming here to visit," I answer, walking over to the window in his office, admiring everyone walking around as if nothing is going on in the world outside of the little safe bubble we allow them to have. "Angelo may be playing both sides, so you need to keep an eye on things," Ademaro stated and I turn, letting the traps fall.

"I know, he was visited the other night with his pants down, literally. I think we have to move up our timetable with buying the votes or making them disappear."

"I don't think that's necessary," Ademaro says, loosening his tie. He's a handsome man standing about five foot eight, with dark brown eyes, short black hair. Square jaw, wide, pointed nose, straight teeth, with a clean-shaven look.

"Well it's good you're not in charge. I think if we don't hear anything by the end of the week we will have to take it a step further in getting what I want. Hate to force people, but I'm determined to make a move on the De Luca Cartel with or without you. I have too much money wrapped in this deal with Antonio's father to let anyone fuck it up," I tell him.

"Queen, why are you so heartless? I mean you have plenty of money, what else do you need?"

Grabbing my purse, I bend over his desk and reach to pull his face close to mine.

"Heartless is such a simple term, I'm not a simple woman. Explaining to you my motives won't help you to understand what I need. So, I suggest you get what I asked you for, or you'll be one of the people missing by the end of this week." I answer, kissing both his left and right cheek.

"Threating a parliament official is a death wish."

"Aren't you glad you're not a real parliament official, you're only playing the role I cast you in. Now be a good little boy and get me my territory signed over before we have a bigger issue." I smile and tap the folder and turn to walk out. "Keep the photos, I have plenty more copies." I'm determined to run the entire Eastern and Southern border from the local police, Italian government, and the Americans. I was born in Italy, my family has deep roots in politics and as soon as Ademaro has played his part as Prime Minister, we'll have our foot in the door, making sure only Vitale product is shipped in and out of Italy.

Now it's time to visit an old friend.

I put my shades on and walk out of the building to my waiting car as security trails behind me.

Unknown: *The package has taken off.*

Me: *Perfect. Set things in motion for a little visit.*

Chapter Nine

Sabrina
    "AJ, make sure you watch your sister while I cook dinner."

"Mommy, why? She's boring and takes all my toys."

I give him the look, narrowing my brows and peering into his eyes and he shuts his sassy mouth and turns back around to watch his sister while I put the groceries away and clean up.

Antonio being gone leaves me with the full responsibility of the kids. But what's new, right? I have to keep them entertained while he's gone otherwise it's a constant barrage of questions about when Daddy's coming home.

You'd think we'd have the kids spoiled. But growing up in my family, and being big on working for what you want, early on I told Antonio that my children would not have things handed to them. He mostly agreed, but he does sneak in special surprises too much sometimes. But I don't bother him about it.

Hearing the doorbell chime has the kids jumping up and excited I left out of the kitchen as the housekeeper opened the door. With our lifestyle, we had private security, but Antonio still had cameras installed after my kidnapping.

"Grandma!" AJ and Jonathan screamed and clapped.

"Hi, my babies." My mother bent down to give them a hug and kiss. Watching her face as she looked them over gave me peace in knowing they had both my parents for support. Antonio's mother is great, but FaceTime calls only did so much. His father is a different situation; I still can't figure him out.

"What are you doing here? Is Daddy here too?"

Shaking her head no, I helped her out of her jacket and hung it up on the coat rack. She picked Jonathan up and kissed his forehead and he ran back off to the living room.

"He's at home and I'd just got off the phone with your sister and wanted to come to see you guys. Where's your husband?"

"Out of town. I'm about to cook dinner if you want to stay and help?" I snapped not intending to be rude, but the little patience I had left was leaving me.

Taken aback she felt my forehead with the palm of her hand and I looked at her crazily.

"What are you doing?"

"Checking to see if you're sick, because no child of mine, no matter how grown will speak to me in that manner. Now, do you want to sit and have a glass of wine and talk about why you are so pissed off?" Mother said opening the cabinet and grabbing two wine glasses.

I went to the wine closet in our kitchen that we had redone once I moved in with AJ and we got married. We had marble kitchen floors, industrial size stainless steel oven, fridge, and counters. Also we expanded my closets and added to the guesthouse for the family if we had visitors.

"Sorry, I'm frustrated with my husband and still trying to make sense of the miscarriage. I partially blame myself, and I somewhat blame Antonio. Is that crazy?" I said opening the bottle and pouring her some, then myself. Sitting across from her at the table we both sipped and savored the sweet blackberry hint in the bottle of red wine.

"No baby, that means you're human and you're still processing what's happened. You know before you girls were born I'd had a miscarriage early on with your father."

"Damn, I'm sorry. I didn't know."

She waved me off and I peeked into the living room and the kids were still laughing and playing as the housekeeper kept an eye on them.

"No one knew because it was just mine and your father's situation. Honey, you don't need to tell everybody your business. Not everyone has good intentions. Anyway, we worked through it and then you and your sister came along."

"I hear you, I guess I expected him to slow down and for things to not get even more complicated in our lives. Opening up more clubs, even hearing the conversations he's having with Carlo about the deals they have set up and the politics behind how our government has a hand in things."

"Focus on your kids and work. Does he want you involved?" Mother questioned.

"No," I answered pouring more wine into my glass.

"Then you need to stop trying to be this mafia wife and simply be his wife. He didn't marry you thinking you'd sit in on his business dealings. I didn't raise you to go around shooting people and getting involved in drug deals." she whispered lowly away from the kids. I giggled at her thinking I was this big-time mafia wife.

"I can assure you, Antonio doesn't have me involved in

any of his dealings. Janice and I steer clear of anything to do with the business."

"Let me stop you right there. You and Janice are mothers now, not twenty-year-old teenyboppers that can go around investigating and sticking your noses where they don't belong. Do I have to remind you about your kidnapping a few years back or him getting shot?"

"We haven't had any major issues in years and my kids are the priority and work. Did Dad tell you I'm taking over as the CEO soon? I have to tell the board soon and he's already moving me into his office." I said standing up to start dinner.

"He did, and I'm super proud of you baby. Stay focused on the long term, giving these kids the best life possible." Mother replied as we continued talking as I made beef stew, corn on the cob, and cornbread.

Chapter Ten

Antonio
"Madre, how are you feeling?" I kissed her cheek as she tried to stand strong with her cane, for the last few years she'd been battling leukemia. She smiled lightly and sat her tea down, and I joined her for lunch. Bruno and Carlo were inside giving us some alone time before we had our meeting with my father and then Angelo was supposed to be here to confirm any details.

"Antonio, you worry too much son. How are my babies and Sabrina?"

"The kids are doing fine, they'd love to see you more. I was hoping to convince you to fly back with me for a visit."

"You know my home is here now and being out of the big city keeps me young." She joked through a hard cough.

"Young and beautiful like always. I believe you can be even more so back in the states running after your grandkids."

"Have you spoken to your father?"

"What is the doctor saying about your diagnosis?"

"Don't change the subject."

"Don't bring him up and I won't, you're more important."

"Tony, Family is all we have, your father has made mistakes."

"Please don't apologize for him. I didn't come here for that, did Bruno tell you Liz is due pretty soon? You'll have another grandchild to spoil soon."

I poured us both more tea when suddenly my phone vibrated on the table. Ignoring the text messages from Sabrina I continued talking with my mother.

"Don't ignore your wife on my account."

"I'll reply back to her later. She probably wants to send me a photo of the kids acting crazy or something, they're always playing on my phone. When we were thinking of getting AJ a phone and we argued for two days straight." I explained.

"He's too young for that Tony, and how is Sabrina handling motherhood with three kids and work? I remember I tried to work when I had you, it didn't last long and your father made me choose." Mother said sighing with a sorrowful look on her face.

"She's working part-time and juggling motherhood well. I tried to convince her to take a little more time off, after losing the baby, but she's just as stubborn as me when it comes to working."

The old traditions in Italy had the wife staying home as the husband went out and worked. Since we're not in the old days anymore, and my wife is a fiercely strong, smart, and driven person. I never saw an issue with her working outside of the home. Honestly, it made me even prouder to be her husband and watch how she not only prioritizes our family, but her love of what she does outside of the home. Her business mindset has always drawn me toward her and knowing she can be just as ruthless in business as me was a turn on. It was one of the reasons I fell in love with her and placing old traditions on new love wouldn't work out for our family.

"So beautiful out today. What time is your meeting? I'd like to have dinner with you boys later if possible."

"In an hour, we can do dinner if you promise to consider coming back to the states with us. I have to get back to Sabrina and the kids before the week is out."

"What about having them come here for a little while? I know AJ would love to play out in the garden, he's into basketball now right, since the last time we talked he asked me to buy him a LeBron James jersey?'

Hearing my mother discuss any type of sports let alone American sports caused a chuckle between us both. "Yeah, he's at that age now where he wants to play different sports, first it was soccer and now it's basketball."

"I'm glad you're letting him be a kid and not forcing the family lifestyle on him Tony. It shows that you're not completely like your father."

"What does that mean?"

She rose up and placed the napkin on the table, I stood to help her with her cane. "It means that I love your father with all of my heart, and the things he's done as your father and Capo I've forgiven because I know he wasn't always like this and you don't see that sweet side of him. Same as Sabrina sees all sides of you that you keep hidden from everyone else. Walk with me inside so I can plan what our meal will be tonight and I'll think about your request."

Walking alongside her with our arms entwined together. She patted my chest and smiled as we strolled through her garden, looking at the roses and lilies she had planted. Gazing at the yard as an adult it didn't feel so big now. Compared as to when I was little. This was the home I grew up in as a little boy and watching my parents have parties, arguments, making up and I'd be in on all of those moments, they were teaching me how to be a man. Many nights I would sit with my father and uncles around the kitchen table, talking about how I would take over one day after my father retired. Rule our family with an iron fist and now all I wanted was to be a normal husband and father.

She slides the patio door open and I let her lead the way inside and down the corridor of our home. The walls still held paintings they'd received over the years from friends of famous artists, stones and vases that my mother collected. We could probably open a museum with the amount of stuff they housed here.

"Go down and talk with your father. Carlo, please keep an eye on him while I get dinner started." Mother grunted sounding out of breath from the long walk into the room.

"Sit down Ma, you don't need to be on your feet."

She waved for me to leave her alone as I ran a hand down my face in frustration. She's stubborn and won't budge when it comes to her health, but if it's anyone else she loves. They had to listen to her demands without question.

"Antonio I'm fine, the chemo is helping, it just leaves me feeling tired and winded sometimes. Now go talk to your father and then come back for dinner." As usual, she got her way and I pecked her cheek and walked off with Bruno and Carlo trailing along behind.

* * *

Bruno set on the couch tapping away on his phone, Carlo stood off to the side watching my father and I stare at each other, neither one willing to speak first. We sat in his man cave that held a gun cabinet, his desk with all of his prized artwork displayed on the walls, a pool table, with a well-stocked bar for when his men came to converse.

"You mind telling me why you're working with our enemies? I thought you knew better than that Father?"

"Don't speak to me like I'm some imbecile boy!" Father exclaimed slamming his hand down on the desk.

"Pop, I'm with Antonio on this, you raised us to look the enemy in the eye and destroy him without any hesitation, now we sit here and get information from our sources that you're working with Ademaro and Queen, and for what? Because we killed your brother for trying to kill your son?" Bruno scoffed in anger and jumped up trying to get in our father's face. Carlo stood in between them both and I stayed in my seat watching for my father's reaction.

"I'm the head of this family and I know what's best, you let her get into your head and now you speak to me as though you're not a part of me. How dare you? Why should I not cut out your tongue?" He seethed through gritted teeth, pointing forcefully over at Bruno.

"I suggest you come to terms with who we married and get over it, because they're not going anywhere. Another thing is your best option is to get Ademaro, and Angelo on the phone so we can discuss terms. De Luca Cartel owns the Eastern borders; and no amount of government interference will stop that. Aren't you the one that set up the long-standing deal that we keep seventy-five percent of all sales with guns, drugs, pills, and property?

He sat back and pulled on his cigar, chuckling at my response. "Figlio, this isn't a game. You don't know all of the tricks I have up my sleeve. I recommend you step aside and let Angelo have the territory in New York and then allow Ademaro to control the territory here, you don't want this life anyway. Besides he's not pussy whipped like you, he can handle the big boy deals we have lined up." Father said sneering at me as he released a puff of smoke.

"Everyone knows Angelo can't be trusted and he plays both sides of the fence. What did he promise you?" Carlo asked quietly from the corner.

"More than you can handle."

I chortled at his response. Standing up I placed my hands in my pockets to keep from hitting my father and being disrespectful. The old me would have gone off the rails if anyone insulted my wife.

"Out of respect for my mother, I won't kill you with my bare hands under her roof. As my father, then you should know what I'm capable of doing old man. Like you said you raised me to be the next leader of the family, and I took it on despite me wanting to leave this world behind. Not only is it in your blood, but it's in mine as well. You're not the only one with tricks up his sleeve, I will be heading upstairs to have dinner with Mother and then make some calls. If you're like me, once I leave here you'll inform your snitch I'm coming after them with guns blazing and to have the full force behind them. I'm willing to die for my family, can you say the same?" I said turning and leaving out. Seeing his face turn red at my admission must have broken his heart because he knew right then that I wouldn't let anyone hurt my wife and kids including my own father. He's the enemy now as we move forward, no longer will I acknowledge what he's let come between us.

Chapter Eleven

A**ntonio**

We stood in front of Angelo as he laid out the evidence about my father meeting with Queen Vitale. He'd flown in late last night and I explained that I wanted to meet early this morning. During the awkward dinner with my mother and father, she said she would be happy to come back to America for a little while, at least until things calm down after we take care of business. I could see her and my father weren't on the same page as they use to be. It was taking a toll on their marriage, his insistence of still being in the mafia at his age. Instead he's up here plotting with my enemies to possibly hurt my wife just to get to me.

"They think I'm feeding you false information, at the same time I'm informing all the lower enforcers, heads of state about protocol if something arises," Angelo explained, sitting back down in the chair in the building we used off the construction site, our family had a twenty percent stake in the business with another mafia family, the Fuertes. What Angelo and Ademaro didn't know was that I called an old friend up to help with handling this business transaction. Joaquin "Ghost" Fuertes, was another son born of a Cartel legacy. Unlike me, Joaquin took his time with killing and stalked his prey, something about his quiet demeanor made people feel uneasy around him, and so they always confessed to what they've done rather quickly.

I was the explosive type and reacted before knowing all the information if it had anything to do with my family. Like right now, Joaquin sat staring silently at Angelo as he talked, he's living in America right now working on a few contracts with our family and I'd asked him to fly out here to help because he's very familiar with Queen and her insatiable thirst for power.

"What was the plan that he had in place? Don't leave anything out," Carlo queried, unrolling the maps of land that we owned and operated, plus subsections that another Cartel family has made a cut of toward keeping violence down.

Angelo leaned over the table pointing at a section marked in green which was the central hub of gang territory between the De Luca and Vitale's gang, operating under the guise of Ademaro's protection.

I'd give it to her she was lucky to have an in with the Prime Minister, because he had a say in what could be imported in or out of certain districts. The upcoming election would be beneficial if they have everyone in their back pockets. I needed Carlo to make some calls and see which side everyone is leaning towards.

"Who's this?" Angelo asked pointing toward Joaquin, I didn't want to show my hand too early and have him brought forth, but Angelo could easily fuck up things if I didn't relay exactly what I had in mind.

"This is the person that will either be your guardian

angel or worst enemy if you don't get the job done correctly," I answered, grasping his shoulders. He cleared his throat and continued talking.

"Well, does he speak? I hate to break it to you, but he looks like a pussy with his pretty-boy looks and fancy tailored suit on. Not only will they not take him seriously, but we'd also get kicked out of the room." Angelo responded.

"Eu te mataria com minhas próprias mãos idot," Joaquin replied, smirking as Bruno laughed shaking his head.

"He's the least of your worries if I don't get a sit down with Queen," I said, right as an explosion went off outside and we all scrambled around to make sure we were covered as shots rang out.

This reminded me of my dream, only this time Sabrina wasn't with us. "Little brother, where you at?" Bruno shouted as I pulled my gun out from behind my back where I had it stuck in my waistband. The door blasted open, I jumped behind the table and started shooting off rounds.

Pop! Pop! Pop!

Carlo and Bruno covered Angelo since we confiscated his guns before he came inside. We didn't trust anyone but our own. Joaquin stood underneath the window trying to gauge the number of people shooting at us.

"I told you she wasn't playing nice. You can't flirt your way out of this Tony," Angelo spat covering his head as bullets sprayed back and forth. The large glass window shattered, and smoke filled the room as Carlo pulled Angelo behind him as everyone followed Sonny to the side door toward the panic room. I'd had it built years ago in case of situations like this and knew the time would eventually come. "How did they know we'd be here?" I mumbled under my breath.

"Motherfucker!" Bruno yelled as we got outside and saw our cars riddled with bullet holes, tires slashed.

"Ccagna, cazzo!" I shouted as rage filled me and ran hot through my veins. I started shooting toward anyone that wasn't on the De Luca Cartel side. Not caring if I lived or died at the present moment.

Before I could get too reckless though, Carlo yanked me back as my last bullet went through a young goon's eye, poor kid couldn't have been more than twenty or twenty-two years old.

"Vattene da me!" I yelled, pushing Carlo back and he gripped me by the neck to calm me down.

"Brother, we have to focus, we need to get out of here, think of Sabrina and the kids." Somehow my breathing became steadier when he mentioned Bella and the kids. I nodded and followed him as we ran toward the next abandoned building to gain cover.

Joaquin was on the phone cursing and yelling. Angelo was pacing anxiously back and forth. Bruno and Sonny stood off to the side watching to make sure no one saw us enter. "Get Padre on the phone, I bet money he's behind this," I told Carlo not believing my father would set me up to die. He was only one next to Angelo that knew we'd had this meeting scheduled.

Chapter Twelve

Queen

I sat in the back of my limousine watching as my team completely surrounded the building Antonio and Angelo were holding their meeting inside. I didn't want my presence announced just yet, and this was the first step in me taking over everything. Ademaro sat next to me rubbing my thigh and I wanted to smack the smile off his face. He didn't do anything but tag along to the show. But he was acting as though this was his idea to get them trapped in a position where they were not able to escape. At first, I wanted to meet in person and discuss a compromise, and then over time I decided to change plans.

Angelo was no longer helpful like Antonio's father is and he gave up his location with very little coaxing, so I decided to spring up with a surprise. Of course, we lost a few men, but that's the price you pay when joining the mafia.

"I can't wait until he sees my next surprise," I said giggling, smacking Ademaro's hand off my thigh.

"We had a deal, scare him to gain a stronger negotiating stance. What else did you have planned Queen?"

Listening to him whine like a little bitch, I tried to rein in my disdain for men being in power with little balls that couldn't do anything right without a woman taking control. "If you must know, his little wife should be receiving a little package as we speak, while she's at work."

"What! That's not a part of the plan, and you know that going after the Capo's wife before we even set up what we want would give him all the advantages."

"Well, plans change, besides I'm not in the mood to negotiate anymore. I want it all," I snapped rolling my eyes and opening the door, slamming it back closed and walking up to one of my men. "They escaped Queen. The buildings are all surrounded so they can't get far." Johan said peering into my eyes. He was in love with me and I felt bad because I only used him for sex. I wasn't what you might call the affectionate type, and when I needed to scratch an itch he was on call. He was tall and sexy, from South Africa with a deep accent, high cheekbones, wide eyes, and broad shoulders. Standing about six-four in height. He wanted more from our relationship, but I kept putting it off and explained that if he couldn't follow my lead then I'd cut him off. After a while, he agreed and only showed affection when it's just the two of us. Unlike now he tried to reach out and caress my cheek. I smacked his hand away, glaring into his eyes.

"Do your job and find them," I replied, walking around him back toward my car. All the men in my life were getting on my nerves today.

Stepping back in the car, I slammed the door as Ademaro rushed off the call he had placed. "Who were you talking to?" I questioned.

"That was one of our contacts in America, I wanted

someone to keep an eye on things since you sent a little surprise to Antonio's wife."

Shrugging my shoulders carelessly the driver started the car and we pulled off as my men continued checking out the building.

* * *

Five hours later, I was home relaxing in my tub after a long day of watching my enemies scramble around chasing who they thought was Ademaro. When the real culprit behind all the bullshit was much more powerful. I had updates on Sabrina and her family's house. I allowed them to continue to live, even though that might cause a little friction with Antonio's father. He wanted her dead, but I wanted to use her for leverage a little longer.

Johan walked in the bathroom naked and I licked my lips, as his thick muscular thighs and long dick that I couldn't wait to have down my throat came into view.

"Are you pleased with how today went my love?" He questioned, feeling a little too comfortable with calling me, love.

"Can you wait in the bedroom, please? I need my alone time after such a stressful day." I responded taking a sip of my wine and leaning my head back.

He didn't like my answer and grunted in response heading back into the bedroom. *Men and their egos.* I thought to myself. Standing up I got out of the tub and dried off letting the water drain out. Looking myself over in the mirror, I smiled ready to begin the era as the new Don of all of Eastern Europe, not just Italy or America. Gaining control will come at a cost, but I was willing to give up the kids and family for what I wanted most out of this world. Money and power.

Chapter Thirteen

Sabrina

"Janice, I'm serious I think we need to go to counseling."

"Like sitting down and telling all your problems to a stranger?" Janice said over the phone. She was off work today, taking care of the twins since they had a cold. Carlo and Antonio were still out of town and we hadn't heard any news. I was optimistic they'd be home today and I wanted to approach Antonio with the idea of us going to marriage counseling.

"Yes," I said moving the papers I had on my desk to the shredder.

"You do realize you are going to have Antonio like that guy on the TV show that couldn't handle being a mobster so he went to see a therapist." Janice joked while CJ screamed through the phone.

"That's not funny."

"Shitttt...seriously you have to admit it's funny what was the name? Uhmm... Sopranos!"

"At times like this I do question our friendship."

"Girl, if you didn't have me your life would be boring. Anyway, when do you plan to spring this brilliant idea on him? I want to be there." Janice answered just as my secretary knocked on my door, not waiting for me to say come in she walks in holding a package.

"Mrs. De Luca, this package just arrived for you and the courier said to open it immediately," Liza said.

"Janice shut up and let me call you back, something just came for me in the mail."

"What is it?" Janice asked.

"Who knows, probably a gift from Antonio."

"Well, open it while I'm on the phone I like surprises.' Janice replied. I grabbed the yellow envelope and asked Liza to close my door on her way out. Placing the phone down on the desk I opened it and a bunch of pictures of my kids at school, home and of my parents fell out.

"Oh my God!" I screamed, jumping out of the seat.

"What! Sabrina, talk to me. What's going on?" Janice rushed out as I heard CJ screaming in the background. I picked up the photos and each one had a circle around it with an x mark over their faces. I grabbed my keys and bolted out of my office. "Janice meet me at my house," I said not caring about anything but making sure my family is safe. I had to call the school first to see if anything had happened as I ran to my car scrambling to get the key in the ignition and not panic.

"Fuck! I forgot my purse." I groaned to myself for leaving my ID behind.

Starting the car and tearing out of the garage, I turned onto the street and drove off toward the school as I dialed Antonio's number.

"Come on Antonio, pick up," I muttered hearing the dial tone. Praying he's alright, I hung up and called my parents. "Hey baby, you never call this early during the day." Mother picked up cheerily.

"Are you and Dad okay?" I asked not caring about traffic lights as I zoomed through the intersection. The bright side is that the school wasn't too far from my office.

"Yeah, we're just at home relaxing before we pick up your sister from the airport, what's going on Sabrina?" I felt a little relief at the same time I cursed because I completely forgot Ashley was flying in today.

"Okay, keep the doors locked and call Ashley and make sure she doesn't talk to any strangers until I can get someone to pick her up."

"What's going on? Let me get your father."

"I don't have time to explain, just stay inside and I'll have security at your house a.s.a.p. Don't answer the door until I call you back with confirmation of who I'm sending." Hanging up the phone I finally made it to the school and parked not caring who I was blocking. Soon as I jumped out of my car and ran inside, out the corner of my eye I saw Janice with Betsy on her hip.

"Janice put the gun away, this is a school they won't let you inside like that."

"If they don't want me going off on and calling my husband to put this entire school on lockdown, they'll open those doors and let me inside." Janice spat with her hands on her hips, popping her lips like a teenager throwing a tantrum.

"I don't have time for this right now." I brushed past her and ran towards my son's classroom. I yanked the door open as everyone jumped in surprise.

"Mrs. De Luca, are you alright?" AJ's homeroom teacher Mrs. Sanders asked. I nodded and walked toward

AJ's desk and he looked concerned. I put a smile on my face to ease the tension and grabbed his backpack.

"Everything is fine, I needed to check AJ out of school early for a family surprise. You can send his assignments to my email address and I'll make sure he gets them done." I exclaimed hugging AJ to my side as Janice walked into the room with Jonathan.

"Mommy, are you okay?" AJ looked up noticing I was putting on a front for the classroom; he could always sense my moods. For a while, it was just the two of us and then came the other kids, but we've always held a close bond.

I bent down and kissed his cheek, whispering I was fine. Janice picked Jonathan up and my phone rang. Noticing my sister calling I answered as we walked out of the building.

"Hey, are you here?" I followed behind Janice to our cars as she strapped Jonathan in his car seat. AJ got in the back and I closed the passenger door changing the phone from left to my right hand to see who was beeping in on the other line. Noticing it was Antonio's mother I wanted to check on him at the same time get my family secure at home.

"I'm here, but Mom said I needed to wait for you to pick me up."

"I'm sending one of our security guards to pick you up, nothing's wrong though so don't panic. Do what he says and I'll call you back once you make it to the house." I hung up before she could question me about anything having to do with me sending a bodyguard. My sister was worlds away from the mafia lifestyle working as a doctor in a level-one trauma center.

"I'm following you to the house. I'll call Liz and see if she's heard from Carlo or Bruno." Janice said, walking over to her car getting inside and waiting for me to pull out into traffic back to the house.

Thinking over my situation that's the first place they expect me to go, so I decided to change it up and headed over to my parents' house instead. Texting Janice the new plan. I started my car and said to follow me over to my parents'. Calling my house security, Jared picked up and I gave him the rundown on what was happening.

"Mrs. De Luca, what's going on? I thought you'd be at work?" Jared said.

Peering at my babies in the backseat, AJ looked over at me with a piercing stare that suggested he knew more at his young age that we'd thought kept carefully hidden and this was the part of our lifestyles I didn't want to expose them to at the same time. It's our reality.

"Jared, we had a breach and I need Maria to bring my baby to my parents' house. I have AJ and Jonathan. Janice dropped the twins off with her parents and is following behind me."

"Say no more." He said hanging up and I released a long sigh. I checked my messages and called Liz to see how she was doing.

Chapter Fourteen

Sabrina

"Carlo, I need you to call me back a.s.a.p.!" I yelled into the phone as his voicemail picked up.

A few minutes later my phone rang with Carlo's name flashing across the screen. "Yeah, Sabrina you there?" Carlo asked.

"What's going on Carlo? I received a envelope of photos at my office about my kids and no one seems to know where they came from."

I hear him sighing on the other end as though something was bothering him and he's struggling to tell me how much I need to know without Antonio getting upset.

"I'm working on getting a security detail to follow you back to the house. Keep your head on a swivel and all will be explained soon." Carlo said and abruptly hung up before I could delve into asking about who sent the photos or Antonio's whereabouts. We parked in my parents' driveway and I finally received a message from Carlo telling me Antonio is fine and they'll call me later tonight. I didn't like not knowing what was going on, if he was in trouble or if I needed to be by his side. AJ helped to get his little brother out of the car right as Jared pulled up with three cars deep of security behind him. Ashley stepped out of the last car and ran towards me and we hugged.

"You hung up before I could get a word in edgewise about the kids. Does this have something to do with Antonio?" Ashley inquired as the door to my parents' home opened and the kids ran to hug my mom.

"Let's talk inside." I say, ushering everyone inside as Maria grabs the baby bags and follows behind my mother.

"I'll fix the kids something to eat and get them comfortable with a movie." Mother explained. I watched Jared hand my baby girl over to my mom walking off toward the kitchen as my father came to sit beside me on the couch. "He isn't answering your calls is he?"

Releasing long tears that finally escaped, I leaned my head on my father's shoulder and he patted my thigh.

"He's in Italy somewhere, with god only knows who, and doing something that's putting him in danger. I need to call his mom back and check on her because she was supposed to be flying back with him."

Janice answered her ringing phone and I perked up and at her mentioning Antonio. "Put him on the phone so I can curse him out for taking this long to reply to his wife." Janice scolded.

"Janice, don't start." Carlo said on the other end of the phone, we heard whispers coming through.

"I'll start and finish if you two don't get some sense. Having us worry and shit. Do you know Sabrina..." I waved my hand for her to shut up before spilling the beans over the phone and getting Antonio worked up.

She sucked her teeth and passed the phone over, a strange feeling came over me, I knew then it was Antonio and he was probably pissed.

"What happened?" Antonio demanded and I walked off to my old bedroom to have a little privacy for the conversation to come.

"Where are you?" I asked closing the door.

I heard a lot of yelling and cursing on the other end that sounded like Bruno.

"I'm fine Bella, how are you and my babies doing?"

Kicking off my shoes I sat with my legs tucked under me and closed my eyes breathing in his voice. Knowing he was okay, gave me some comfort until I could see him in person.

"When are you coming home?"

"I'm flying out tonight with my mother after we finish up some last minute things here."

"I received a package at the office today with photos of the kids and my parents with circles and x's drawn across them like they're meant as target practice," I answered with a low sniff, trying to not cry and get upset.

"This is a type of situation I wasn't expecting and I apologize for not being with you Bella. It won't happen again, Queen and my father have tested my patience for the last time."

Hearing a woman's name I perked up, wanting to know who the hell she was. "Queen? What does she have to do with your father, is he cheating on your mother or does he really hate us so much that working with an enemy is better for his bloodline?"

"She's the daughter of Frederico Vitale and she's trying to take over our territory in America and here in Italy. Padre cut a deal with her to get a piece of the profits and we got ambushed."

She sucked her teeth and passed the phone over, a strange feeling came over me, I knew then it was Antonio and he was probably pissed.

"What happened?" Antonio demanded and I walked off to my old bedroom to have a little privacy for the conversation to come.

"Where are you?" I asked closing the door.

I heard a lot of yelling and cursing on the other end that sounded like Bruno.

"I'm fine Bella, how are you and my babies doing?"

Kicking off my shoes I sat with my legs tucked under me and closed my eyes breathing in his voice. Knowing he was okay, gave me some comfort until I could see him in person.

"When are you coming home?"

"I'm flying out tonight with my mother after we finish up some last minute things here."

"I received a package at the office today with photos of the kids and my parents with circles and x's drawn across them like they're meant as target practice," I answered with a low sniff, trying to not cry and get upset.

"This is a type of situation I wasn't expecting and I apologize for not being with you Bella. It won't happen again, Queen and my father have tested my patience for the last time."

Hearing a woman's name I perked up, wanting to know who the hell she was. "Queen? What does she have to do with your father, is he cheating on your mother or does he really hate us so much that working with an enemy is better for his bloodline?"

"She's the daughter of Frederico Vitale and she's trying to take over our territory in America and here in Italy. Padre cut a deal with her to get a piece of the profits and we got ambushed."

"Your father set you up to get killed?" I shouted as Janice walked into my room and stood pacing back and forth.

"We made it out Baby. I'm with Bruno, Carlo, and Joaquin now, we're heading over to Ademaro's office. I just got word they're both there." Antonio answered.

"I'm coming to you now. The kids will be fine to stay with my parents."

"No."

"What do you…"

"This has nothing to do with you and I'd rather not have another kidnapping situation. I can handle myself, but I'd worry if you're here."

"I don't like this Tony, what if they're setting you up again once you make it to his offices?"

"One thing I can promise is that I'll always come back home to you Baby."

"You can't promise me that."

"I love you, Sabrina De Luca."

I smiled at him saying my last name even though he couldn't see my smile I felt his arms around me.

"I love you too Antonio. Be careful and make sure to kill that bitch."

He chuckled at my words and we hung up at the same time, lying back across the bed. I sighed and crossed my arms over my eyes to keep the tears at bay.

"We do have access to your father's private jet." Janice boasted giving me something to think about.

"He's right, if we went out there it would only cause confusion and worry. We have to trust they'll cover each other's back and get home safely.

"You are stronger than me," Janice said sitting down next to me on the bed.

"What do you mean?"

"I never listen to Carlo, and Antonio has you wrapped around his fingers. I would have been on the next flight wreaking havoc with Betsy if some woman tried to kill my man." Janice says kicking off her shoes.

"I forgot to ask, what are you wearing under that housecoat?"

She lifted the collar of her coat and grinned. I shook my head already knowing she was probably naked underneath.

'Carlo should have you committed."

"Only if he commits himself. I can't be away from my on-call dick for more than one day." Janice chortled and I threw a pillow at her.

"OMG! I swear you have no good sense."

"Welcome to Janice's world," she said, referring to herself in the third person.

Antonio

Chapter Fifteen

Antonio

The next day after we escaped the shoot out we regrouped at Joaquin's home. He had Angelo under lock and key as I set up a plan to get into his offices and cut the vote before it happens today. If we have to spill a little blood along the way then so be it, I needed to get home in one piece and I could hear the frustration in Bella's voice. The last thing I needed was her giving up on us and my nightmares becoming reality, with some one threatening my wife and kids they would see the wrath I draw upon where I leave no stone unturned. I would wipe out entire bloodlines if I get a hint of someone doing something to harm Sabrina.

I got out of the car, grabbing a gun from Bruno as we walked up the stairs of Parliament. It was early morning before a full vote could be cast and I got word my father and Ademaro were here now. Angelo didn't have a gun on him, so we had him walk in front of us. His best plan was to duck if shit started going down; otherwise he was a dead man walking.

"Antonio, you're walking into a government building and they don't allow guns. I suggest I go in and talk with them about a possible negotiation." Angelo tried to stop us from entering, looking around nervously as we were nudging him along, we entered the building and security stood up and I nodded for Bruno to take care of them and he shot them with his 9mm, just a slight pop was heard from the silencer as both security guards slid to the marble floor.

Joaquin had his team on standby and they locked the surrounding buildings down as though construction was happening during this hour. We all wore hard hats and gear. Passing another hall we came to Ademaro's door and heard whispering coming from within the office.

Angelo was about to knock and I nudged him to the side kicking the door open. Ademaro jumped back screaming as I shot in him in the arm. Shaking my head in disappointment as I watched my father sat stoically with a cigar in his mouth in front of the desk looking like he didn't have a care in the world, then I observed a woman I assumed was Queen Vitale perched on the corner of the desk smiling.

"Wait...fuck, I didn't have anything to do with this!" Ademaro yelled.

"Antonio, we finally meet. I'm Queen Vitale." She reached her hand out for me to shake and I pointed my gun at her face.

"I didn't ask for your name, and I suggest you sit with your hands clasped in front of you before I blow your fucking head off, bitch!" I seethed through clenched teeth.

"Figlio, have a seat." my father said teasingly, inviting for me to sit in the seat across from him as his pulls a cigar out of his pocket, clips the end and offered me one. I shook my head no and focused on the woman in front of me.

"You must be Carlo and you're Bruno," Queen said

sitting on the edge of the desk with her legs crossed.

"If you weren't so evil and I wasn't married I would have you sucking my dick instead of running a man's business." Bruno spat out.

She laughed and pulled out a cigarette from the silver case next to her, about to light up.

"Didn't you come here to negotiate? We both want money and no more bloodshed. I apologize for the other day and the ambush that my men started without my permission. Johan can be a real go-getter." She taunted, winking and puffing on her cigarette.

"De Luca's don't negotiate, we keep things the way they are and you get to live," I said not giving her any time to reply as I shot Ademaro in the head.

Pop! Pop!

"You just assassinated a fucking Prime Minister Tony," Carlo said walking over to check if he had a pulse.

"Like I said, De Luca's don't negotiate," I replied and she nodded her head and I watched as her bodyguard pulled a gun from behind his back and shot my father in the head.

Pop! Pop!

He fell out of the chair with his eyes still open. Bruno screamed and I watched as Johan grabbed Queen from behind to take her to cover. Bruno ran toward my father and I watched Carlo shoot Angelo in the leg to keep him from running away. Nothing about that could help my father and having to take on the role of telling my mother that her husband wasn't coming home would be hard. On top of her dealing with her illness, we'd have to plan a funeral, but he chose this life and died by the rules he taught me. If anyone ever violated the oath of the De Luca Cartel they'd have no choice but to die at the hands of the Capo. Him being my father of course, gave me pause, because bringing pain upon my family isn't something I want. Letting his traitorous ways go unpunished would only send a message to the rest of our enemies and fellow Cartel members that I'm weak. The only time I'll be weak is when I'm on my knees for my Bella.

* * *

Three hours later, after cleaning up the room and making sure there was no evidence was left behind, I had the all the security footage erased, and we packed up my mother and were on our way back to the US. I couldn't wait to be back in Bella's arms and see my kids, knowing I could have been taken from them if my father would have gotten the deal implemented. Madre slept in the bed at the back of the plane crying herself to sleep, once we arrived back home and she saw all of the blood she knew her husband wasn't walking through those doors ever again. Burying him in the states was her only request so she'd be able to visit him whenever she wanted. Her doctor said she was cleared to fly, as her cancer was officially in remission and she had gone through her last chemo treatment so she could travel. I had already called Sabrina with a little surprise, and she was excited to move into a new home that I had our realtor find. Only thing I wasn't thrilled about was talking to a therapist, she forced attending marriage counseling on us to help us navigate the grieving process and the distance we had been experiencing in our marriage after losing the baby. I felt it wasn't something normally suggested in the Cartel lifestyle, opening up to people outside of your direct family, or members in the same business. At this point I'm willing to do anything to show Sabrina it wasn't a mistake to start a life with me. The distance between us was partially my fault and I want to close the gap.

Chapter Sixteen

Sabrina
Two months later

He was not a happy camper today and I knew sitting in this office would not make it any better. Now that things have died down with everyone trying to kill him and our family. I forced him to come to counseling, to talk about everything that has happened over the past year. The therapist we decided to hire didn't know all the details of our lives, but she did understand that we're a high profile couple, so discretion was guaranteed.

"So Mr. De Luca, how do you feel about therapy?" Dr. Gordon asked quietly taking notes on her tablet.

Antonio looked as though he didn't know how quite to respond and I stared back not letting him get out of this until we came to terms with how things are going to be moving forward. His father wasn't a factor in our lives anymore, after so many years of dealing with him trying to destroy us, it was like a fresh start for us. My mother in law moved here, to be close to all of her grandchildren and Antonio wouldn't admit it, but I knew he was still dealing with the trauma of watching his father get killed. I didn't pry or question him about his business, but once he came back from Italy he seemed different. More on edge, walking around constantly checking the locks on the windows, he was on the phone more with Carlo and Bruno, and they were not talking business about the clubs. Antonio would always smile even when things were crumbling around him, lately his attitude and demeanor was guarded, like a wall was built up. I recall asking him if he was going to work on upcoming events at Ryde for the re-launch in New York and he told me he had someone else managing his clubs for the time being.

"Fine," Antonio answered, flicking a piece of imaginary lint off of his slacks.

"Is that it?" Dr. Gordon questioned him.

"Extremely fine."

"Antonio you promised to take this seriously! We both lost people in our lives and you're sitting here like a statue." I explained.

His cold eyes peered at me and a chill ran down my spine. I knew that look all too well, he was shutting down unless I forced his hand. "Do you want to become like your parents? Because that's where this is leading if you continue down this path." I could tell he didn't like that answer and blew a harsh breath out.

"Sabrina, this isn't easy, you and I come from different worlds." He replied.

"I didn't ask for you to pursue me!" I shouted, standing up and grabbing my things to leave when he gripped my hand pulling me down into his lap.

"Sabrina, just let him get it out. Interrupting only causes confusion." Dr. Gordon explained.

"What I was going to say is that with us coming from

different worlds it never dawned on me not to love you. I couldn't walk away from you after that first moment years ago. You were meant for me and I was meant for you. My father was a complicated man, but his ideas of what or who I should be married to never crossed my mind." Antonio said running a hand across my face, wiping away the tears falling down my face.

"Baby, I don't blame you for the miscarriage, and I hope you don't blame yourself. It happens, no matter what we couldn't have prevented this outcome."

I moved out of his hold and sat next to him, intertwining our hands. "You're right, a part of me was blaming you and then everything that happened with the pictures and you not calling me back when you're away. I get nervous and scared. Yes, I'm stronger than before, but sometimes your lifestyle is overwhelming."

"I think this was a great start to a longer conversation. Can we get a commitment of you two coming together once a week for counseling?"

Leaving the ball in Antonio's court I waited to hear his answer. Nothing will be resolved in one day and after two months I was still getting used to security following my every move, even more so than before. Queen went missing and to ease my nerves Antonio had my parents, kids and I tasked with twenty-four-hour security. We've moved into a bigger home in a gated community, and the kids would be driven to and picked up from school by Sonny personally.

"Anything to make my Bella happy," Antonio said, kissing me on the lips as we stood to leave.

* * *

It wasn't even a full hour after leaving the therapist's office and Antonio pulled over to the side of the street and leaned over to kiss my lips. I saw the lust in his eyes, we haven't had a moment alone in a while and after the funeral of his father, finding Angelo dead. His leadership was needed in the illicit business more than his club business these days. Our quality time as husband and wife had been put on the back burner until now.

"Come here," He motioned for me to get in his lap, I was grateful I wore a skirt today because dressing and undressing in a car was not always the sexiest thing to do.

"Shouldn't we wait to get home or maybe a...hotel?" I pecked his lips, running my tongue across his bottom lip.

He slid my panties to the side and unzipped his pants, I lifted my hips and eased down on his shaft as we both moaned into a kiss.

"Uhhh...Bella...shit." Antonio hissed, slowing moving me up and down.

I unbuttoned my blouse and Antonio ran his tongue across my breast and used one hand to pop them out of my bra. "Keep going baby." I encouraged as our thrusts picked up.

"Fuck! I love you so much, Sabrina." Antonio growled into my chest as his grip tightened around my waist.

"I...Yessss...Oh. My. God!" I screamed as his pace picked up and I accidentally hit the horn as I stretched my leg out to get a better angle. "You and I belong together forever."

Antonio bit my nipple, smacking my ass and squeezing as we both continued to meet each other's thrusts. "I want another baby!" I screamed out as he popped my breast out of his mouth as looked at me intensely.

"Are you sure? Because I'm happy with our family now, and I don't want you to be disappointed if it doesn't happen."

Understanding his statement I deepened our kiss and

tightened my walls around his girth. He moaned into my mouth and we came together. "Ahhhh!" We both said as our bodies shuddered in the aftermath of a powerful orgasm. As our breathing slowed down and we held onto each other, not moving from this moment.

Chapter Seventeen

Queen Flashback- The day of the shooting

Johan and I ran down the back stairwell of the building and through the back alley. I look around and notice only one man, probably part of the cleaning crew unloading supplies with a van running. We couldn't go back toward the front of the building and risk getting caught. I grab his gun, as he's leaned over catching his breath. Checking over my shoulder to make sure no one is watching or coming down the alleyway. He followed behind me as the music blaring from the van blocked out any conversations. I tapped the janitor on the shoulder.

"Hey beautiful."

Smiling in his face, I bring the gun from behind my back and shoot him between the eyes with no remorse.

Pop! Pop!

Still pissed I shoot him again in the stomach, letting off three more shots from the silencer.

"Queen we need to get out of here." Johan said, trying

to snatch the gun out of my hands. Pushing him away I raised the gun in his direction and he froze.

"What the fuck just happened?" I hissed pointing the gun right in the middle of his forehead.

"Put the gun away, we need to get out of here and regroup." Johan says shaking his head lowering his arms. He didn't understand what the recent setback would end up costing me in the long run.

Closing then opening my eyes. I breathed in deep and lowered the gun off Johan. Out of everyone in my life he's been the most loyal. Jumping into the van we drive out as more police cars pull up, along with ambulances. As we get further away, I see a few unmarked cars passing us. Rolling the windows up and sinking down in my seat, I allow my eyes to slide closed again to think of how everything went so horribly wrong.

Present Day

It was all over the news the day of the shooting. Local police had everyone on lockdown with all the Cartels on notice. Former Don of the De Luca Cartel getting killed wasn't a small thing. Following my escape with Johan, we'd been holed up in my father's childhood home in Southern Italy together. His family kept this place up even though I didn't frequently visit. After Johan killed Antonio's father, and watching Angelo get killed, I needed to regroup. All of the people that I used in my plan to get on top were getting killed off one by one. Sleeping with a gun underneath my pillow was a normal routine and getting payback on Antonio was my life's ambition. I wasn't Camilla, Alex, or even his traitorous father. Antonio didn't care about getting killed and that was my mistake. I needed to take the one thing he lived and breathed for. *"Sabrina Washington."* I whisper to myself as the local news shows a picture of

Sabrina, and an older man, more than likely her father, based on the resemblance standing at a press conference.

I hear the sound of a car door slamming; I step over to the window checking to make sure it's Johan. The darkness overshadowed my vantage point and I couldn't tell if he was alone. I hear a key in the door, right as I'm checking the chamber of the gun preparing to head to the front door, it suddenly fly's open. "Who sent you?" I spat, not showing any fear.

A smirk graced their face as a hand reached out gripping my neck. Kicking and screaming to get out of his tight grasp as more men pick me up by my legs.

"Fuck you!" I shout continuing to fight and claw my way out of their hands. They open the doors of the truck as Johan lies dead in the driveway with a single gunshot to his head as something covers my nose and mouth and the darkness overwhelms me.

Antonio

Sitting in my office at Ryde, I was waiting on Carlo to show up after dropping Janice off at work. I'd planned to leave here early and have a home-cooked meal with Sabrina and the kids in our new house. For Queen to have access to where my kids laid their heads and went to school gave me pause. I needed to make a few changes and one of those changes was moving my family, her parents, and sister that now lived here into the same gated community. We haven't spent that much time together but we briefly talked over breakfast once I came back into town and picked everyone up from her parents' house. Sabrina wanted another baby and I wanted one too, at the same time the last few months in our lives caused me to think twice, and I can't go through another miscarriage and possibly cause a larger riff in our marriage that we both won't be able to come back from. Therapy was a starting point, to fostering healing. Divulging my fears and lifestyle wouldn't be a good thing if my enemies got a hold of our secrets. However, I made a promise to try and I will for the time being, I'd do anything if it brings us back to the place we once were happy and carefree along with our family.

A knock on the door resounded and without waiting for my reply Carlo walked inside, plus Bruno holding his son. "Liz actually let you out of the house with the baby?" I stood up walking over to grab my nephew out of his arms and kissed his chunky cheeks. Seeing Bruno as a father was different as seeing him as the enforcer of the crew. He made it a priority to spend weekends with Liz and his kids. Something I was also starting to do more of as they got older.

"Fuck you, I run my house." Bruno sat down on the couch in my office and Carlo sat in the chair looking exhausted.

"What's got you looking worn out?"

"Janice and her sex drive, that woman will not leave me alone since we've been back in the states." Carlo bragged, not wanting to sound like a wimp for not telling his wife no.

Bruno and I burst out in laughter as a frown flashed across his face.

"That shit's not funny. Anyway, have you heard from Joaquin?" He asked.

Jimmy started spitting up and I grabbed a baby wipe out of my desk, I was fully prepared since Sabrina often came down here during the day if she had a break and complained about not being able to freshen up properly. She stocked my office with baby wipes, and other necessary supplies, plus we brought the kids here to hang out sometimes.

"We've texted and he's planning on coming to visit soon. Work is keeping him tied up."

"How is counseling going? I told Janice it might be good for us to see someone." Carlo exclaimed.

We all dissolved in laughter at the mention of Janice and seeing a therapist.

"Don't laugh at my baby. She's a special one, but honestly, how are you dealing with your father's death? I went to visit your mom the other day and she wasn't doing too good."

Sighing in annoyance at the mention of someone asking about my grief over what happened to my father. He would have been the cause of me losing my sweet Bella and I couldn't find it in me to cry over him. Telling something like that to Carlo in front of Bruno though would only cause more problems than I needed. Bruno was closer to our father when we were younger, and back before the Cartel took over our lives with me getting picked over him as the Don of the family. He was taking the loss a little harder that I was and there were many nights that Liz called asking me to keep an eye on him. Bruno can be a hothead at times, and anyone that pisses him off would probably end up dead for the smallest infraction while he's grieving over our father's death and betrayal.

"Have you visited his gravesite?" Bruno stared at me intently as I handed his son back over to him. Picking up my phone and noticing a message from Sabrina I smiled returning her text.

Wife: *I love you.*

Me: *I love you more, Baby.*

"I will when I'm ready. Have you taken care of Angelo's body like I asked?" I replied not letting the conversation go any further and effectively changing the subject.

"Yeah, he won't be missed after a little acid got into his system and the casino is closed until further notice," Bruno answered.

Angelo was a thorn in my side and him being a witness to us killing Ademaro would only come back to bite us in the ass. I needed to take care of all the loose ends.

"Good, so run down where the next shipment is coming in and see where we have the most inventory," I ordered as we continued talking business for the rest of the night. A few minutes later Sabrina stopped by and dropped off dinner and grabbed the baby to take him back to Liz. We kissed as I led her out of my office.

"Don't be too late," Sabrina moaned, stealing another kiss as she sashayed out of my office.

Chapter Eighteen

Antonio
One month later.

The sun was setting perfectly as we all gathered on the beach to renew our vows. I told Janice to coordinate with local authorities to block a part of the beach off for our privacy during the wedding. As a high profile couple and after the death of my father, I didn't need things getting back to Italy and someone new thinking I'd gone soft again. Plus, this wasn't to make up for missing our actual anniversary, I wanted to do something to show Sabrina and our kids that I was here and nothing would come before them. Janice helped to plan everything and as we stood in front of our families and friends on the beach I couldn't imagine anywhere more perfect. Sabrina wanted something more intimate for the renewal of our vows, so we comprised on this location in California. AJ was my best man standing beside me in his matching tuxedo, along with Jonathan, and our baby girl was the flower girl. My mother sat next to Sabrina's parents trying to conceal her grief and wipe the tears she still experienced from the aftermath of my father's death.

"Do you Sabrina take Antonio to be your lawfully wedded husband again?" Pastor Donovan asked as we stood in front of everyone.

"I do."

"Do you Sabrina take Antonio as your wedded husband, to have and to hold in sickness and in health till death do you part?"

"Yes!" The kids yelled out before she could answer, everyone laughed as Sabrina and I shook our heads in embarrassment.

"I do."

I tightened my grip on her hands as we stood face to face staring into each others eyes, she wore an off white gown with a lace bodice and a long mermaid train. She had little diamonds embedded across the waist with our names engraved. Her hair was up in a veil hanging off the back and small diamond studs in her ear.

"I now pronounce you husband and wife again. You may kiss your bride." Pastor Donovan responded and everyone cheered as we held each other not moving just holding her close, bending down to lay a sweet kiss on her lips.

* * *

"Move your fucking hands, Bella," I demanded as I lifted her leg in the crook of my shoulder easing my dick in slowly. She was so wet, and warm it drove me crazy. I didn't care about the dinner reception. I needed to be inside her. We let the kids go off with her parents and Sonny was standing by if anything happened.

"Tony, you're so deep. Oh...wait," Sabrina tried pushing

me back. I grinned looking at her beautiful face contorted in a sexy smile.

"What's that about another baby Bella, huh?" I pulled out, slapping the tip of my dick against her sweet, sexy mound. Teasing her as her juices continued trailing down her leg and onto to the sheets. She gripped the linens as I sank back into her, pounding as the headboard started making noises. Luckily everyone except our personal security, who knew not to interrupt, was outside drinking and having fun. We could go as many rounds as we wanted to without any possible interruption.

"I can't...Mhmmm," she bit her lower lip. I leaned over as sweat dripped off my brow. Licking her from her navel up to her chest, I reached for her hands to clasp together. We kissed and her leg tightened around my waist.

"I love you," I whispered in her ear, my orgasm was quickly approaching and I was not ready to cum. I slipped out and motioned for her to turn around and get on her knees. A newfound respect and passion ignited my attention on my wife and I made not only a promise to her, but also to myself, to never let her feel as though she's not the most beautiful woman in the world to me.

Before slipping back inside I licked from her ass to her pussy slipping my tongue inside as her juices lingered on my tongue.

"So sweet Bella." Her entire body shivered, as her breathing became uncontrollable.

"Don't pass out on me now," I said smacking her ass.

"Right there." she said, looking over her shoulder and reached out pushing my face further between her pussy lips. Leaning up I watch as she runs her other hand around her front gripping her breasts, pulling her back to my chest, gripping her by the neck gently and easing my tongue inside her mouth and dick back into her pussy. Taking another hand playing with her clit. I continued our lovemaking until we both came with a moan, jerking inside her, knowing this was the one. Bliss fell over both our faces as we fell into a deep sleep.

Chapter 19
Epilogue

ne Year Later.

"He looks just like you Bella." Antonio said, leaning down next to the chair in our new baby's room. Little Luca was a surprise for our family. We stopped forcing it and just let nature happen. One night I felt a flutter in my stomach and weird smells that caused me to vomit. We made an appointment with the doctor for the very next day and she told me I was pregnant.

"His hair is so soft, Amore Mio." Antonio ran a hand across Luca's cheek, up toward his dark curls. We peered into each other's eyes and he leaned up to kiss me on the lips. I was still a little sore from giving birth, plus having three other kids that needed my attention and a crazy husband to keep up with. Luca slept peacefully in my arms and I buzzed him close to my nose, breathing him in as he yawned with his little lips moving and his eyes drifted closed.

"Is this everything you ever wished for Antonio?"

"More than I could ever imagine Sabrina. Ever since you stepped into my world, I felt a need to keep you protected from harm, at times even me. I'm a selfish man, possessive, and the second you walked into my nightclub that night. The moment our eyes met and my heart started racing I knew that was it. I realized that living on this earth without you would be the death of me. If I'm being honest, you'll never hear me apologize for loving you, that's something that can't be undone. Letting Sonny, Carlo, and Bruno take care of all major decisions on the business front has been made official with all our contacts. Spending more time with you and the kids is all I want, but you know in this business I'll never be completely out."

"That's what's worrying me. I find myself thinking of the boys and even our baby girl wanting to follow in their Dad's footsteps. Already AJ picks up on your attitude and temper. I'm worried about him." I explained placing Luca in his crib, moving his blanket over his shoulders. Antonio stood and wrapped his arms around my waist as I released a long sigh in contentment.

"Mr. and Mrs. De Luca, the kids are ready for lunch in the dining room." The newly hired nanny peeked her head into the room and said. At first, I was against having more help around the house, but with four kids and Antonio at home more. I wanted to balance being a wife and mother, along with time alone for myself. Often someone was calling on me for something. After much discussion and debating, he hired an older woman that his mother recommended. She was about fifty years old, with grown adult children of her own, and was only here during the daytime.

"We'll be right down Miss Celeste." Antonio said over his shoulder as he buried his face in my hair, squeezing me tight with my back to his chest.

"AJ will be fine, Bella. I won't become my father; he will make his own choices in life when he gets older. Now let's go down and have lunch with our babies, then I want you to feed me." Antonio whispered with a growl.

"No sir, you have six weeks to wait before we can have sex," I informed him as he turned me around to look at the scowl on his face.

"Rules are meant to be broken, Baby." Antonio pleaded as he reached a hand up and caressed my cheek.

"They are and look at what the rules got you, four kids and a wife that won't let you fuck her until the six weeks are up. Now let's go hang with our babies."

$$* \ * \ *$$

Get into more Antonio and Sabrina in **Redemption Book 5** https://books2read.com/u/b5kZ8O or a One night-stand romance with **Renew Book 4** https://books2read.com/u/4NXyPG

Heart of Stone Book 3.5 https://payhip.com/b/HGP1

If you want more "Mafia Romance, why not try **"Antonio and Sabrina Book 2" Click here** https://books2read.com/u/bpED6g

Have you read *yet* **"Temptation?** That is a stand-alone contemporary, sports, curvy girl romance. Check it out here https://books2read.com/u/mle1Vv

Are you interested in Mafia romance? Check into

Antonio & Sabrina: Struck in Love, Books 1 https://book
s2read.com/u/4AxKLo

***

Check out **Aydin a grumpy boss, bodyguard romance** here https://books2read.com/u/mBwaOy .Follow my standalone opposites attract, age gap, military romance "**Exposed**" https://books2read.com/u/bQyYZe .

Are you a fan of sports romance? Then download one-night stand, billionaire romance "**Refuel**" https://book s2read.com/u/boDyDA. Also, follow it up with workplace, sports romance "**Pressure**" https://books2read.com/u/ 3Ly1r7 .

If you love romantic comedy, fake relationships, enemies to lovers, find it here, "**Something Gained.**" Click the link https://books2read.com/u/baGLYy .

Any fan of forbidden romance, political? Check out "**Mutual Agreement**" https://books2read.-com/u/mgzzWX a steamy romance. Pre-order the full novel of "**Nasir**" here click the link here.

Have you checked out "**She's All I Need**" click here https://books2read.com/u/49lkeW a sports, opposites attract romance. What about dark romance that has everything from steamy romance, opposites attract, suspense, thriller, celebrity, and more "**Joaquin Fuertes Book 1**" https://books2read.com/u/mvZlgV

Catch up with favorite characters in this holiday short romance which includes spoilers. https://books2read.com/ u/bzd59G

Sneak Peek: Joaquin & Sofia

As the son of Joaquin Fuertes, the longest running Mayor in Portugal, and founding father of the Fuertes Cartel, he had groomed me to run the family business with an iron fist. I was known as the Ghost because I'm good at making problems disappear. The young lady sitting across from me in a chair as her forced nod of agreement told me I had failed to convince her to do as I requested. A deep frown crossed my face. This bitch was looking to destroy not only the De Luca Cartel, but ours as well here in Italy. Queen was known as a hard ass, and Antonio had made it clear to not cross him again or her entire bloodline would be wiped out. I stepped out of my chair as she sat with tape wrapped around her mouth keeping the screams at bay, blood dripping down her body from numerous injuries.

She was given the chance to leave when Antonio confronted her back at the meeting. Afterwards, she continued on with her plan and Antonio agreed for me to put an end to her plans. Both the De Luca and Fuentes'

Cartel had an agreement that as long as we made money together we wouldn't interfere with each other's territory.

I'm not an abuser, unlike other men in the Cartel. I had my ways of getting what I need out of my enemies. Raising my sleeves on my crisp white shirt, stepping forward as my enforcer Gabriella continued the ritual of cutting off one finger at a time when you didn't comply and answer my questions. I didn't need to have a gun on me like my counterparts.

I've lived in Italy for the past two years and recently an opportunity came up for me to visit America, more specifically the Big Apple, for a business exchange that would extend the Fuertes Cartel territory in the underground illegal dealings.

"Take the tape off, Gabriella."

"Joaquin, you don't want to do this. We can forge a new deal and I can get you all the territory you need plus guns. Your father isn't the only one with ties in America." Queen said weakly, trying to convince me to betray my father. Not wanting to hear anymore of her lies, I winked and Gabriella smiled knowing this was the signal to end her life. As she prepared to have fun, I gathered my jacket off the chair and walked out of the back of Antonio's, the restaurant was a front for the De Luca Cartel, even though it was the top celebrity spot for politicians. Everyone knew what happened here. As Queen's screams finally died down. I walked up the stairs and opened the door. I bumped into a soft body and before we both fell I gripped her by the waist.

"Ohh...Excuse me."

A light sweet smell invaded my nostrils. Our eyes connected and my grasp grew tighter. "Hello, you can let me go now." She said with a chuckle, as we both leaned against the wall away from the restaurant.

"Joaquin, the car is here and Gabriella texted you. What's going here?" Monica pointed between me and the mystery goddess in my grasp that I somehow can't make myself let go of. I was only trying to prevent her from falling down, and my eyes never left hers, something about them kept me hypnotized.

"Mira a donde vas hermosa?"

"Huh?" She asked as I grinned at the perplexed look across her face, dropping my hands from around her waist. Monica followed behind me and passed my phone over as Gabriella texted the package was cleaned up.

Gabriella: *The package is secure.*

Me: *Inform De Luca and let him know we should have dinner plans while he's here.*

Gabriella: *Any other guests?*

I looked back over my shoulder as the woman I just bumped into headed toward a seat that a man pulled out for her. A strange feeling came over me and I couldn't explain it as she peered up and caught my eye. Turning away, I opened the car door and got inside, ignoring whatever odd feeling came over me from being in her presence.

"Joaquin, are you listening to me?" Monica asked sitting beside me in the limousine, rubbing a hand over my thigh.

"Not right now Monica." I said moving her hand off my thigh and focusing on texting Gabriella back.

Me: *My Father.*

To be continued in 2020, a new spinoff (Joaquin and Sofia Untitled Series)

Heart of Stone Series

Heart of Stone Book 1 Emery and Jackson
https://books2read.com/u/boWPAV
Heart of Stone Book 1.5
https://payhip.com/b/kWg7
Heart of Stone Book 2 Jordan and Damon
https://books2read.com/u/ba2OMx
Heart of Stone Book 3.5 Bottoms Up
https://payhip.com/b/HGP1
Heart of Stone Book 3 Angela and Brent
https://books2read.com/u/31rx9l
Heart of Stone Book 4 Jessica and Joseph
https://books2read.com/u/4NXyPG

Struck In Love Universe

The Early Years-A Prequel
https://books2read.com/u/49Zjnw
Ruthless Struck In Love Book 1
https://books2read.com/u/4AxKLo
Savage Struck In Love Book 2
https://books2read.com/u/bpED6g
Beast Struck In Love Book 3
https://books2read.com/u/3LpgdJ
Janice and Carlo Captivated By His Love
https://books2read.com/u/b6je6M
Brutal Struck In Love Book 4
https://books2read.com/u/4NQyE9
Stolen-Fuertes Mafia Cartel Book 1
https://books2read.com/u/mvZlgV
Saved-Fuertes Mafia Cartel Book 2
https://books2read.com/u/4DWwLd
Redemption Struck In Love Book 5
https://books2read.com/u/b5kZ8O
Betrayal- Fuertes Mafia Cartel Book 3
https://books2read.com/u/4A5LGp

304 Publishing Company

We showcase authors writing African American, Interracial, Women's Fiction, Urban Romance, Erotic, and Contemporary Romance novels. Along with Thriller, Suspense, Poetry, Beauty, and Style Books. Thank you for taking the time out to visit. Join our mailing list to stay updated with new releases and blog posts.

Spotify Playlist

"Antonio and Sabrina Struck In Love Series"

1. Heather Headley- In My Mind
2. Love on the Brain -Rihanna
3. Cockiness -Rihanna
4. 7/11- Beyonce
5. Crazy In Love- Beyonce
6. Radioactive- Imagine Dragons
7. When We- Tank
8. Insecure- Jasmine Sullivan
9. Ain't Too Proud to Beg- The Temptations
10. You Keep Me Hanging On-The Supremes
11. Be Without You- Mary J Blige
12. Fire and Desire- Rick James & Teena Marie
13. I'd Rather Go Blind- Etta James
14. Make You Feel My Love- Adele
15. Lost Without U- Robin Thicke
16. Apologize- One Republic

About the Author

Chiquita Dennie is an emerging author of romance. This is her seventeenth book, and Award winning Filmmaker. Her first short film "Invisible" released in Summer 2017 and screened in multiple festivals and won for Best Short Film. Also, she hosts a podcast that showcases the latest in Beauty, Business, and Community called "Moscato and Tea." Her debut release of Antonio and Sabrina: Struck In Love has opened a new avenue of writing that she loves.

Chiquita lives in Los Angeles, CA. Before she started writing contemporary romance, worked in the entertainment industry on notable TV shows such as: Dr Phil show, Tyra Banks show, American Idol, and Deal or No Deal. But her favorite job is the one she's no doing full time, writing romance.

If you want to know when the next book will come out, please visit my website at http://www.304publishing.com, where you can sign up to receive an email for my next release.

Catalog Releases

The Early Years-A Prequel Short Story
    Antonio and Sabrina: Struck in Love 1, 2, 3,4,5
    Heart of Stone, Book 1 (Emery & Jackson)
    Heart Of Stone Book 1.5 Emery &Jackson A Valentine's Day Short
    Janice and Carlo: Captivated By His Love
    Heart of Stone, Book 2 (Jordan and Damon)
    Temptation
    Heart of Stone, Book 3 (Angela and Brent)
    Bottoms Up Heart of Stone, Book 3.5(Jessica and Joseph Short
    Cocky Catcher
    Bossy Billionaire
    Love Shorts:A Collection of Short Stories
    Joaquin Fuertes (The Fuertes Cartel Book 1)
    Exposed (Salvation Society Novel)
    Joaquin Fuertes (The Fuertes Cartel Book 2)
    Refuel(A Driven World Novel)
    Pressure(A Driven World Novel)

Until Serena(HEA World Novel)
Exposed (Salvation Society Novel)
Heart of Stone, Book 4 (Jessica and Joseph)
She's All I Need
Something Gaine(Romantic Comedy)

WHAT'S NEXT?!

Want to know what happens next?

Follow me on Amazon to catch the next release.

Reviews are the lifeblood of the publishing world. They're read, appreciated, and needed. Please consider taking the time to leave a few words on Amazon, Goodreads, or Bookbub.

Sign up for updates and sneak peeks at the site below. wwwchiquitadennie.com

www.ingramcontent.com/pod-product-compliance
Lightning Source LLC
Chambersburg PA
CBHW011202190726
48286CB00009B/2886